PRAISE FOR
The Year of the Dog

*"Lin does a **remarkable** job capturing the soul and spirit of books like those of Haywood or Maud Hart Lovelace, reimagining them through the lens of her own story, and transforming their special qualities into something new for today's young readers." —*Booklist*, starred review

"A **charming** first novel, an autobiographical tale of an Asian-American's girl's **sweet and funny** insights on family, identity, and friendship....Lin creates an endearing protagonist, realistically dealing with universal emotions and situations. Girls everywhere will find much to embrace here." —*Publishers Weekly*

"A **heartwarming** story." —*BookPage*

"This comfortable first-person story will be **a treat** for Asian-American girls looking to see themselves in their reading, but also for any reader who enjoys stories of friendship and family life." —*Kirkus Reviews*

"The story, interwoven with several family anecdotes, is entertaining and often **illuminating**. Appealing, childlike decorative line drawings add a delightful flavor to a gentle tale full of humor." —*The Horn Book*

"**Strong** in the classic virtues of accessibility and warmth." —*The Bulletin*

The Year of the Dog

A novel by

Grace Lin

LITTLE, BROWN AND COMPANY
New York · Boston

Little, Brown and Company
Hachette Book Group
1290 Avenue of the Americas, New York, NY 10104
Visit us at LBYR.com

Originally published in hardcover by Little, Brown and Company in December 2005
Paperback Reissue Edition: January 2018

Little, Brown and Company is a division of Hachette Book Group, Inc. The Little, Brown name and logo are trademarks of Hachette Book Group, Inc.

The text was set in Humana and the display type was set in Kristen Normal and Kentuckyfried

The Library of Congress has cataloged the hardcover edition as follows:
Lin, Grace
The year of the dog / by Grace Lin.—1st ed.
    p. cm.
Summary: Frustrated at her seeming lack of talent for anything, a young Taiwanese American girl sets out to apply the lessons of the Chinese Year of the Dog, those of making best friends and finding oneself, to her own life.

  ISBN 978-0-316-06000-4 (hc) / ISBN 978-0-316-06002-8 (pb)
  1. Taiwanese Americans—Juvenile fiction. [1. Taiwanese Americans—Fiction. 2. Schools—Fiction. 3. Chinese New Year—Fiction. 4. Family life—Fiction. 5. Contests—Fiction. 6. Theater—Fiction.] I. Title.
PZ7.L644Yea 2006
[Fic]—dc22

                                        2005002586

ISBNs: 978-0-316-06002-8 (pbk.), 978-0-316-03097-7 (ebook)

Printed in the United States of America

LSC-C

Special thanks to:

MY MOM,
who gave me her stories and 14 photo albums dragged out of storage

MY DAD,
who laughed when he read it, so I knew it must be good

MY SISTERS, LISSY AND KI-KI,
who let me put them in even though I didn't make them
as beautiful or as smart as me

MY HUSBAND, ROBERT,
who told everyone this was my best book ever even before he read it

and

MY SCIENCE FAIR PARTNER, ALVINA,
who grew up and became my editor

Chapter 1

A Sweet New Year

ring ring ring

"HAPPY NEW YEAR!" DAD LAUGHED INTO THE phone. "Gong xi-gong xi! Xin-nian kuai le!" The phone had been ringing all night with relatives calling to wish us a happy Chinese New Year. If we had lived in Taiwan, we would be having a big dinner with all of our relatives—aunts, uncles, and cousins. But since we lived in New Hartford, New York, they called us instead.

"Yes," Dad said over the phone to Uncle Leo, "happy Year of the Dog!"

"What does it mean when it's the Year of the Dog?" I asked. Our kitchen was full of rich, heavy smells because Mom and Lissy were cooking the special Chinese New Year dinner. I was teaching Ki-Ki how to draw a dog for our decorations. "I know every Chinese New Year is a different animal, but is

Pacy is probably good at drawing

something special supposed to happen because it's the Year of the Dog?"

How to draw a dog

^{1} ς ^{2} ς ^{3} ς0 ^{4} ς0 ^{5} ς0 ^{6} ^{7} ^{8} ^{9}

"Yes," Lissy told me, nodding her head so hard that her black hair swung back and forth. Lissy always thought she knew everything. "You know how they say a dog is a man's best friend? Well, in the Year of the Dog you find your best friends."

"That's true," Mom said, her hands mixing speckled brown meat, "because dogs are faithful. They say the Year of the Dog is the year for friends and family. But there's more to it than that. The Year of the Dog is also for thinking. Since dogs are also honest and sincere, it's a good year to find yourself."

"Find myself?" Ki-Ki said. "Why? I'm not lost."

We all laughed and Mom tried to explain.

"No," she said, "finding yourself means deciding what your values are, what you want to do—that kind of thing."

"Like deciding what you want to be when you grow up?" I asked.

"Yes." Mom nodded her head.

"Well," Lissy said, "I've decided I'm definitely NOT

2

going to be a chef, because I'm tired of cooking. We still have to make the shrimp, the pork, and the vegetables. We're never going to eat!"

"We will, we will," Mom said, and she looked at the clock. "Pacy, stop drawing and go fill the New Year tray."

I went to the cabinet and took out the New Year tray. We had polished it so much that I could see myself shining in the red and black wood. I also took out a bag of the special Chinese New Year candy. It's very important that the New Year tray is filled with candy. If it's full of sweet things, it means your year will be full of sweet things.

Ki-Ki hung up our drawings and then came over to help me, though she didn't really help much. All she did was eat the candy. She loved New Year's candy. I don't know why. It isn't *real* candy like chocolate or lollipops. New Year's candy is sticky taffy melon candy, the color of the moon.

Ki-Ki kept eating the candy, so I couldn't fill the whole tray. I looked in the cupboard for more, but there wasn't any more. But there were rainbow-colored M&M's. I loved M&M's. That's real candy. So I filled the rest of the tray with that.

New Year Tray

When Lissy saw the tray, her mouth made a big O.

"You can't fill the tray with M&M's," she told me. "It's a Chinese tray; only Chinese candy is supposed to go in it."

"But there's not enough Chinese candy to fill it," I told her.

We both looked at the tray. We couldn't decide if it was better to have the tray be half empty with only Chinese candy or full with Chinese and American candy.

Mom was frying food, so we took the tray to Dad. He scooped up a big handful of Chinese candy and M&M's and ate it.

"This way is good," he said. "We should have both Chinese and American candy for the new year. It's just like us—Chinese-American. I think it's going to be a very sweet year!"

our house

Chapter 2

How to Get Rich

the fish

vivid descriptions

"TIME TO EAT!" MOM CALLED.

In the dining room, there was so much food. There was a whole fried fish—crispy and brown, meat dumplings fried golden, vegetables shining with oil, steamed buns that looked like puffy clouds, shrimp in a milky sauce, and pork colored a brilliant ruby pink. The fish's eyes stared at me. I didn't like it, so I turned that plate around so it would look at Lissy instead. She turned it back toward me. And I turned it again. Finally we had it look at Ki-Ki. She didn't notice.

"Everything we eat tonight has a special meaning," Dad said. "These vegetables mean wealth."

"How about the shrimp?" I asked.

"That means wealth, too," Dad said.

"What does the pork mean?" Lissy asked.

"Wealth, too!" Dad said.

"Everything means wealth," Lissy said. "All we care about is money!"

"Well, don't you want to be rich?" Mom asked.

"Yes!" Lissy and I said at the same time. Ki-Ki nodded her head.

"I want to be a millionaire," I said.

"I want to be a gazillionaire," Lissy said.

"Me, too," Ki-Ki said. "Me, too."

"Well, eat these," Mom told us, passing us the fried dumplings. "They say these symbolize gold coins, so if you eat them you'll be rich."

fried dumplings

"I don't know how they're going to make me rich," I said. "They don't look like gold coins to me."

"Maybe that's what coins looked like in the olden days," Lissy whispered to me.

"I'm going to eat all of them," Dad teased, "then I'll have all the money and you'll have none."

"That's not fair," I said, trying to grab some dumplings off his plate. "Give me some."

"I'll sell you one for a dollar," Dad said. "That's how you get rich!"

The phone rang again and this time it was Grandpa calling to say Happy New Year.

"I bet Grandpa ate a lot of these dumplings," Lissy said. "Grandpa's rich."

"Maybe he charged two dollars for each dumpling!" I joked.

"Actually," Mom said, "Grandpa got rich by doing a job for free. Did I ever tell you the story about Grandpa's first patient?"

We all shook our heads and Mom started the story.

HOW GRANDPA GOT RICH

When Grandpa graduated from medical school and was officially a doctor, he was so proud! But he had a problem. He had no patients. It seemed like whenever people were sick, they went to someone else. No one wanted to go and see Grandpa, a young doctor with no experience.

Still, with the help of his parents he opened a small clinic in the neighborhood. Sometimes his mother would come over saying she had back pains so he could cure her. Sometimes Grandpa would use the stetho-scope on himself, just to make sure it was working. But most of the time, Grandpa just sat there alone, like the last dumpling on a plate.

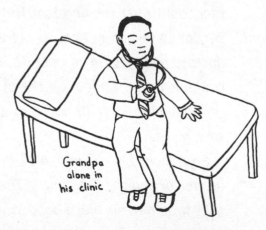

Grandpa alone in his clinic

Then, one night, just when the sky began to darken with shadows, there was a frantic banging on the door. A street vendor had been robbed and was badly hurt. His clothes looked like dishrags of blood, and his wife begged for help. Grandpa jumped up and worked hard to save the vendor's life. He worked deep into the night, and he only stopped when the moon hung like a freshly peeled lychee in the sky. Finally, the patient was out of danger. Grandpa left him with his wife in the clinic and told them that he would check up on them in the morning.

But, when Grandpa woke up the next morning and went to check on his patient at the clinic, there was no one there. The bed was made and the room was as clean as an empty rice bowl. Had he dreamed it all?

Later, Grandpa found out that his patient was very poor. He and his wife had sneaked away after Grandpa had left because they knew they could not pay him. In fact, right after the accident the wife had brought the vendor to two other doctors before Grandpa; the other doctors had refused to operate because they knew he couldn't pay. Grandpa, on the other hand, didn't even think about asking for payment and had just hurried to save his life.

So it looked like Grandpa's first patient was going to be free of charge. Grandpa worried because he thought that it didn't look like a good start for his business. He had his family to support and they were counting on him to make money as a doctor. Was this first patient a sign of his future?

But he shouldn't have worried. Like the smell of roast pork, the news of Grandpa's good work spread around the village. People were warmed by the fact that Grandpa cared more for their lives than their money. They stopped seeing their other doctors and came to him instead. Soon he had more patients than he could handle.

"And that is how Grandpa became rich," Mom finished. Then she looked at the empty table. "Ai-you! There's no food left for me!"

empty bowl

Chapter 3

Welcoming the New Year

red envelope

AFTER DINNER, MOM GAVE US OUR *HONG BAO* — special red envelopes, the color of a fully bloomed poinsettia, with money in them. Mine had $5! That was a lot of money, but not enough to make me rich. Lissy got $10 since she was older.

Then, Mom got us ready for bed. Ki-Ki had her own room and her own bed, but she never slept the whole night there. She always got up in the middle of the night and went to go sleep with Mom and Dad. Lissy and I shared a room. Our room was buttercup yellow, with flowers dancing on the walls. The carpet was a bright blue, so I liked to pretend it was the ocean and swim to the bunk bed. Lissy slept on the top bunk because she was older and Mom was afraid I would roll off in the middle of the night. But I didn't like sleeping on the bottom. What if the bed broke and Lissy came crashing through? Lissy would be okay, because she'd be on top, but everything would crush me.

"Traditionally," Mom told us as she was helping Ki-Ki put on her faded sky-colored pajamas, "you are supposed to stay up as late as you can on Chinese New Year. The longer you stay awake, the longer your parents' lives will be. So I should try to keep you up all night! But tomorrow is school, so everyone goes to sleep."

Mom putting on Ki-Ki's pajamas

"Aren't you worried?" I asked. "We should stay up so then you can have a long life."

"Yeah," Lissy said, "let's stay up late! We don't have to go to school tomorrow."

"No school!" Ki-Ki chanted. "No school!"

"Sillies," Mom said, "everyone is going to sleep early and everyone is going to school tomorrow."

But after she left, I worried. What if I went to sleep too soon and gave Mom and Dad a short life? If I stayed up an extra minute, would they live an extra year? Or just an extra day? "Don't go to bed yet. Let's stay up," I said to Lissy.

"Okay!" Lissy said. But I could tell she was thinking more about staying up late than Mom's and Dad's lives.

We turned on our bed lights and Lissy took out her book. She was reading *Mary Poppins*. It was very different from the Disney movie we saw. In the book, Mary Poppins is really grumpy. But the characters have better adventures. They even see a circus in the stars. I wondered why they didn't put that in the movie and Lissy said it was probably because it was too hard to make the animals glitter.

I opened my book. It was called *B is for Betsy* and it was about an American girl going to school. I liked it very much, but I couldn't stop thinking about what Mom said about the Year of the Dog and how it was the year I should think about what I wanted to do when I grew up.

"Lissy," I asked, "what do you want to be when you grow up?"

"I'm going to be a doctor," Lissy said, "like Dad and Grandpa."

"I don't know what I want to be," I said.

"You should be a doctor, too," Lissy said. "You can get rich by being a doctor."

"Can't you get rich by being something else?" I asked. "Movie stars are rich."

"You can't be a movie star," Lissy said. "You have to be beautiful to be a movie star. You're not pretty enough to be a movie star."

I stuck my tongue out at her, but since she was in the top bunk she didn't see.

"Besides," she continued, "you have to have acting talent to be an actress. You better pick something you have some talent in."

"How do I know if I'm talented at something?" I asked.

"I don't know," Lissy said carelessly. I could hear her turning the page of her book. "Maybe if you won an award or something."

"But I've never won anything," I said.

"Well, maybe you'll win something later," Lissy said. I could tell she wasn't really paying attention to me. "There's lots of time."

That was true. I had a whole year to figure things out. I watched the stars light up like a string of Christmas lights while I thought about what the New Year would bring. When I heard Lissy snore, I turned off my lamp and went to sleep. The Year of the Dog was here.

Night Sky

Chapter 4

Talent

rice porridge

SOON MOM WAS SHAKING ME AWAKE. MY EYELIDS felt as heavy as sacks of rice.

"Wake up, sleepyhead," Mom said, "You'll be late for school."

"No," I mumbled and tried to turn over.

"Wake up! Wake up!" Mom said, pulling me up.

I sat up, but groaned. "I'm too tired to go to school," I said.

"You're just too lazy," Mom said, teasing me. "Get up!"

So, before I knew it, I was getting dressed and brushing my teeth. I went downstairs to have breakfast. Mom put a bowl of watery rice porridge and flaky dried pork in front of me. I yawned.

"Do I have to go to school?" I moaned.

"Yes," Mom said, "how else will you learn things?

Besides, you shouldn't start off the Year of the Dog as a lazy dog."

"Will school teach me what I'm talented at?" I asked. Mom mentioning the Year of the Dog reminded me about finding myself.

"Yes," Mom said, "I'm sure it will."

"No," Lissy cut in, "it won't. You have to have talent to discover it. You don't have any!"

I opened my mouth to retort, but a yawn interrupted me.

"I'm too tired to go to school," I said again.

"Better wake up!" Ki-Ki chanted. "Better wake up!"

"Yeah," Lissy said, "don't fall asleep in school."

Mom poured me a glass of juice and laughed. "Did I ever tell you about the time I fell asleep in school?"

MOM SLEEPS IN SCHOOL

In Taiwan, school was different than it is here. School wasn't just to teach you about reading and writing; it was supposed to teach you how to be a good citizen as well. Every Monday, there was a school assembly. All the students had to wear their special uniform—a seaweed-colored jumper, shirt, and hat. It had to be clean and unwrinkled and as stiff as a piece of new cardboard. Then, in these uncomfortable uniforms, we had to stand outside in the courtyard while the principal, the vice principal, and the guidance counselors gave long and important speeches. They would tell us how crucial it was that we follow all the rules and work hard. It was so boring.

One day, we had an extra-long assembly. Not only were the principal, the vice principal, and the guidance counselors speaking, but they had a special guest. He was from the government and was going to lecture about how we should always do what we were told and not question authority. It was a hot and sticky day; the sun was like an egg yolk frying in the sky. The hundreds and hundred of students stood like an army of ants. I stood at the very back, lost in the ocean of black heads.

At these lectures, no one was allowed to whisper. Like soldiers listening to orders from their captain, we had to stand up straight, with our hands at our sides, giving the adults our absolute attention.

But when the guest speaker spoke, his voice was so soft. I couldn't understand what he was saying. It was a low, mumbling swaying in the courtyard. To me it was like a lullaby. My eyes started to droop, my head nodded, and then suddenly I was asleep.

When I woke up, I was alone in the courtyard, except for a teacher glaring at me with her hands on her hips. I had fallen asleep so soundly that I was still standing *there when everyone had gone inside. They had just left me there, standing asleep!*

Mom sleeps in school

"The teacher was so angry with me. She put a big mark next to my name and I was so embarrassed," Mom finished, "but I never fell asleep in school again."

"You could sleep standing up?" I asked, now wide-awake.

"I could fall asleep anywhere," Mom said. "I was very talented."

Chapter 5

A Surprise

school lunch

TO GET TO SCHOOL, LISSY AND I HAD TO WALK down the street to the bus stop. Next year, Lissy wouldn't be going to the bus stop with me. Lissy was almost a teenager. Next year she would go to junior high school on a different bus. Then I would be the only Chinese girl in the whole elementary school.

But I'm not really Chinese either. It's kind of confusing. My parents came from Taiwan. Some people thought Taiwan was part of China. So then calling me Chinese was kind of correct. Other people thought Taiwan was a country all by itself, so then I should be called Taiwanese. It didn't help that my parents spoke both Chinese and Taiwanese.

"So when people ask me what I am, what am I supposed to tell them?" I once asked Mom.

"You tell them that you're American," Mom told me firmly.

But my friends didn't call me Chinese, Taiwanese, or American. They called me Grace, my American name.

One of my friends at school was Becky Williams. Becky was tall, with hair as brown as tree bark. At recess, I told her that it was the Chinese Year of the Dog, so we drew dogs on the ground with chalk. I taught Becky how to draw a dog just like the ones I drew for our New Year's decorations.

drawing dogs

"What does it mean when it's the Year of the Dog?" Becky asked. "Does that mean Scruffy gets to boss me around? Maybe he'll eat at the dinner table and I'll have to eat on the floor."

I laughed, but I didn't know how to explain it.

"Chinese people give every year an animal sign," I tried to explain. "You know how horoscopes use animals for some months? Well, for Chinese people it's for every year."

"When is it the Year of the Unicorn?" Becky asked. "I love unicorns."

I shook my head. "I don't think that there is a Year of the Unicorn."

Becky looked really disappointed, so I tried to think of something.

"But maybe during leap year or something they have a Unicorn Day."

"Really? What do they do on Unicorn Day?"

"Um," I scrambled, because now I was completely lying, "they draw pictures of unicorns and hang them up. Sometimes there's a parade."

"Cool!" Becky said, excited. "Will you tell me when that day is? We can celebrate it."

"Okay," I said, but I hoped that by the time a leap year came she would forget all about it.

Like an alarm clock, the bell rang and we lined up to go into the cafeteria. It was spaghetti day! Yum! I loved spaghetti, even though I always thought it was strange that they served it with an ice cream scoop. The spaghetti always looked like tennis balls on my plate.

But when I went to take my plate, the lunch lady stopped me.

"Hey," she said, "I just saw you. You already took a lunch. Everyone only gets one!"

"No!" I said. "I didn't. This is my first time."

"Yes, you did," the lunch lady said. "You took spaghetti and french fries."

"No," I said, "I didn't get anything."

"Are you sure?" the lunch lady said. "I know it was you."

"It wasn't!" Becky said. "Honest."

The lunch lady gave me a lunch, but I could tell she didn't believe us. She kept shaking her head and looking at me suspiciously.

When we went to sit down, Becky nudged me.

"Look over there," she said, pointing. "That's why the lunch lady thought you already got your lunch."

I looked where she was pointing and I saw a girl that looked Chinese, just like me! I hadn't noticed her before because she had been all bundled up in a fuzzy scarf and hat. She was brand new. I couldn't wait to meet her.

new friend

A New Year, A New Friend

Unicorn

BECKY AND I SAT NEXT TO THE NEW GIRL. SHE smiled at me.

meeting Melody

"Hello!" she said. "Are you Pacy?"

"How did you know?" I asked.

"My mother told me about you. My mother met your mother last week. Didn't you know?" she said. "She said there would be another Asian girl in school."

Grace=Pacy

"Her name's not Pacy," Becky said, pointing at me, "it's Grace."

"Grace is my name at school," I rushed to explain. "My mom calls me Pacy."

The new girl frowned and looked a little confused but said, "Well, anyway, my name's Melody Ling."

"Ling!" Becky said. "That's like Grace's last name — Lin."

Melody nodded. "Except it's with a 'G.' L-I-N-G."

We found out that Melody and I had a lot of things that were almost the same. While I had an older sister and a younger sister, she had an older brother and a younger brother. We both had long black hair, but she had bangs and I didn't. We both played the violin, but I was in Suzuki Book 3 and she was in Suzuki Book 2. We both couldn't write in Chinese, but she could speak it and I couldn't. My birthday was May 17 and Melody's birthday was July 17.

"You're almost twins!" Becky said. "Lucky!"

"My mom must have forgotten to tell me about you," I said. "Probably because it's Chinese New Year."

"Yeah," Becky said, "it's the Year of the Dog! Grace is going to tell me when it's the Day of the Unicorn so we can celebrate that."

"Day of the Unicorn?" Melody said. "There's no Day of the Unicorn."

"Yes, there is," Becky said. "It's during a leap year, and there's a parade and we hang pictures. Grace said so."

Melody looked at me and I felt myself turning red.

"I must have made a mistake," I mumbled.

"Oooh," Melody said, "that Day of the Unicorn. I forgot. My family doesn't celebrate it, so I didn't remember. But, you're right, it's a big festival."

Melody grinned at me and I smiled back. I knew we were going to be good friends.

celebrating the
Day of the Unicorn

Almost Twins

Vitamins

WHEN I CAME HOME FROM SCHOOL, I COULDN'T wait to tell Mom about Melody. But, of course, she already knew all about it. Mom told me how she had gone grocery shopping and was surprised to see another Asian woman doing the same thing. The woman was so happy to see another Asian person that she went up to Mom and introduced herself. Melody's parents were from Taiwan, too! So we were both Taiwanese-American. Mom said she would take me over to see Melody's new house.

Moms meeting

It was fun going to Melody's house. She had the best room. One whole wall of her room was a picture of jungle animals. There was a lion staring in the grass and monkeys climbing the trees. There was even a pink flamingo.

"How did you get your wall like that?" I asked, impressed.

"It came that way, "Melody said. "If you look close you can see that it's a kind of wallpaper, not painted."

I looked really closely and I could see a tiny line down the side. It was like a huge ceiling-to-floor poster. We tried to draw all the animals in Melody's notebook. I couldn't copy the lion very well, but Melody thought my elephant drawing was exactly like the one on the wall. Melody's brothers, Benji and Felix, came in and drew,

my drawing

our drawing

too. We drew Melody riding the giraffe and Felix swinging from a vine. Benji and Felix weren't too bad, for boys.

After Benji drew himself feeding bananas to the monkeys, he said, "I'm hungry, let's go get some real bananas."

That's when we realized we were all hungry, so we went downstairs to eat.

In my house, Mom always had cookies or chocolate or cheese and crackers in the cupboards. If we didn't have those, there was always fruit in a can that I could eat, too. But Melody didn't have any of those things. Mom told me Melody's mother was very "nutritious." So in her cupboards there were only plain rice cakes that tasted like paper. There were nuts that were still in the shells and didn't have any salt on them. But there weren't any bananas.

"Don't you have any candy?" I asked.

"No," Melody said, "but we have vitamins. They're kind of sweet."

So we opened the big jar of vitamins. There was a big letter C on them. They were thin and flat and tasted like oranges. They were pretty good. Not as good as candy, but still yummy. We all sat on the floor, eating vitamins.

Melody's mother came into the room and was surprised to see us around the vitamin jar. She seemed a little upset with us. I didn't know why; I thought she would be happy that we were being so healthy.

"What are you doing?" she said. "You shouldn't be eating vitamins like that!"

"We were hungry," Melody said.

"Well, it's almost dinnertime," she said. "I'll make you something better to eat. Pacy, why don't you call your mother and see if you can stay over here for dinner."

I called Mom, and we went back to Melody's room.

"My mom called you Pacy," Melody said. "Your mom and your sisters called you that, too. But everyone at school calls you Grace. How come?"

"Oh, I have two names," I told her, "an American name and a Chinese name."

"Why don't they just call you one of them?" Melody asked. "Don't you get mixed up?"

"Well, " I said, "it was like this . . ."

How My Name Changed from Pacy to Grace

On my first day of school, the teacher asked me, "What is your name?"

Right away, I said, "Pacy Lin!"

But she looked at her roster and shook her head. She said, "No, no, no. You're a big girl now; you don't go by that name anymore. It says here your name is Grace."

I didn't understand, but I just nodded my head. I knew I shouldn't tell the teacher she was wrong, but I kept thinking she had made a mistake. Maybe the teacher had me mixed up with another girl and I was supposed to be somewhere else. Maybe she was me and I was her. How could I find her?

On the bus ride home, I asked Lissy about it.

"Oh, those are our American names," Lissy told me. "They call me Beatrice. Mom and Dad gave us American and Chinese names. I think the people at the hospital told them to when we were born."

"Well, I want to be called Pacy," I grumbled.

"Don't be stupid," Lissy said. "Pacy is too weird for everyone. They won't know how to say it. If I used Lissy they'd ask, 'Is that LEE-SHE or LI-SEE?' And then they'd ask, 'Why do Chinese people always have to have these weird names?' Just let them call you Grace."

I still wasn't convinced. "People won't know which one is really me, though."

"Look," Lissy said, "'it's like egg foo young. At home we call it foo yung don, but at the restaurants they call it egg foo young. So it's easier for Americans to say. But it's still the same egg pancake—you know what you're eating when Mom gives it to you, don't you? And you know what to order at the restaurant. It's not that hard."

egg foo young

"So now," I finished, "everyone at school calls me

by my American name and everyone at home calls me by my Chinese name."

"Well," Melody said, "I guess it's kind of cool. It's like a nickname. But do you want me to call you Pacy or Grace?"

I thought a moment. "I call myself both names," I said, "and we're almost twins. So, you can call me both, too."

Chapter 8

Dinner at Melody's

rice cooker

FELIX CAME INTO THE ROOM AND TOLD US DINNER was ready. I was glad because my stomach was grumbling. "What's for dinner?" I asked.

"Chinese food, of course," Felix said. "The same as your house, probably."

When we got downstairs, I wasn't surprised to see Melody's mother opening her rice cooker. We had rice every day at our house, too. But Melody's mother was scooping out big spoonfuls of BROWN rice. We never had brown rice at my house, only white rice.

And then on the table, the vegetables weren't stir-fried and the tofu didn't have any shiny sauce on it. Everything was plain and colorless and dry.

"Are you sure this is Chinese food?" I asked Melody.

Melody's mother heard me.

"This is Chinese food cooked a healthy way," she told me. "It's very good for you. Try it, you'll like it."

I tried it, but I didn't like it. To me, the rice was too crunchy and chewy and the vegetables and tofu were tasteless. Yuck! I looked at Melody, Benji, and Felix. How could they eat this?

But they didn't seem to think it was that bad. They put everything in their mouths and swallowed it. I just kept pushing the rice from one side of my plate to the other.

"Aren't you hungry?" Melody asked me.

"I thought I was," I said to her, "but I guess not."

Melody's mother looked at me, worried. "I hope eating all those vitamins didn't make you sick."

Could a person get sick from eating too many healthy things? Maybe I was already so full of nutritious things from the vitamins that my body couldn't take any more. Maybe that was why the dinner tasted so bad to me.

We had dried apricots for dessert. They looked like shriveled orange mushrooms. I only had one. By that time, I was convinced it was because my body couldn't fit in any more nutrition, but Melody's mother worried

dried apricots

that it was something else. She called Mom and talked to her for a long time in Taiwanese.

Mom came over and picked me up right away. She put her hand on my head and said that I felt okay, but she'd bring me home just in case.

In the car she said, "It's too bad you got sick; it sounded like you were having a good time."

"It was fun," I said, "but can Melody come over to our house for dinner next time?"

Chapter 9

Red Eggs

window cleaner

MELODY AND I BECAME BEST FRIENDS. LIKE TWO chopsticks, we were always together. She came over to my house or I went over to hers. One day, she came over to help color eggs. They were for my cousin Albert's Red Egg party. He was just born, so we were going to visit him in New Jersey.

When you go to a Red Egg party, you have to bring red eggs. Red eggs symbolize good luck for a new baby. I guess the more red eggs Albert got, the more luck he'd have. I'd get sick of eating all those eggs though.

How to color an egg red

① dip a red envelope in warm water

② rub the moist envelope on the egg

③ the red from the envelope will color the egg red

Coloring eggs red was fun. Lissy, Ki-Ki, Melody, and I dipped lucky red envelopes in warm water and then rubbed the red coloring onto the eggs. Lissy got red dye on her nose and I laughed at her.

Lissy with red dye on her nose

"Is there such a thing as a red egg colorer?" I asked. "That would be a fun job."

"No," Melody said, "there aren't enough Red Egg parties for you to do that for real. Americans don't have Red Egg parties."

"But Chinese people do," I said. "Every time a Chinese baby is born, there's a Red Egg party. Maybe that would be enough."

"Not all Chinese babies get Red Egg parties," Lissy said. "You didn't."

"I didn't? Why not?" I asked.

"Probably because you didn't deserve it," Lissy said. "You were the worst baby. You cried all the time and then you got SO sick. They took you to the hospital and Mom and Dad were so worried. They had to put a tube on your ankle and put you in a plastic box."

Lissy went to go wash her hands and get some paper to wrap the eggs in.

"Gee, what did you have?" Melody asked.

"I know," Ki-Ki piped up. "You got sick from ammonia. Mom told me."

"Ammonia?" I said. "Isn't that the stuff in window cleaner?"

Melody and I looked at each other.

"You must have been allergic to it," Melody said.

"But, we have window cleaner now," I said. "I saw it in the closet."

We went to the closet and looked at the bottles. The bottles were on a shelf, lined up in a row. The window cleaner was in the middle and looked like a bottle of swimming pool water.

"There it is," I said.

"You better not touch it!" Melody said. "You might get sick."

"It must be a mistake that we have it," I said. "Maybe my mother forgot I was allergic to it."

"I'll throw it away for you," Melody said, reaching for it.

"What are you guys doing?" Lissy asked us.

"We're getting rid of the ammonia so Pacy won't get sick again," Melody explained.

Lissy started to laugh. She snatched the window cleaner from Melody and looked at me menacingly. "Are you afraid of AMMONIA?" she cackled, aiming the spray bottle at me.

"Stop!" Melody screamed. Ki-Ki screamed, too, and I started to run. Melody tried to grab the window cleaner away from Lissy, and I hid behind the sofa.

"What is going on here?" I heard Mom say. I crept out from behind the sofa.

"Lissy was going to spray me with the window cleaner," I said. Melody nodded in support.

"Lissy, put the window cleaner away. And you," Mom said to me, "why are you so scared of window cleaner all of a sudden?"

"Because it has AMMONIA," I said and told her the whole story. Mom laughed and shook her head. Then she explained to us that when I was a baby I had had pneumonia, which was like a very bad cold. It was a very different thing from ammonia.

"But if you were allergic," Mom said, "it was very nice of Melody to try to keep you from getting sick."

"I guess you almost saved my life," I told her.

Melody grinned, but whenever anyone mentioned window cleaner after that, we both turned red from embarrassment.

Melody and me

Chapter 10

Albert's Party

cooked duck

MELODY WENT HOME AND WE PACKED UP THE eggs and all our suitcases into the car. Then, Mom made us get all dressed up in our fancy Chinese clothes. My dress was dark parsley green; it felt smooth and cool like a polished jade statue. Lissy's dress was peacock blue, and Ki-Ki wore a pink dress with flowers embroidered on it. The dresses were all silky and shiny and had collars that buttoned close around our necks. The tight collars made it hard to breathe, but I didn't say anything because then I would be acting like a baby, like Ki-Ki. Mom had to leave her collar open because she fussed so much.

Finally, we got in the car and drove to

me in my dress

Ki-Ki in her dress

Albert's house. He lived far away, so far that I got to miss school! We didn't have to travel as far as Grandma and Grandpa, though. They were coming all the way from Taiwan to see Albert. But they didn't go to school, so it didn't matter.

It was a long drive. Sometimes I steamed up the window with my breath and drew a dog with my finger. I tried to think about what I wanted to be when I grew up, but nothing came to mind. Lissy and Ki-Ki just snored.

Sometimes we listened to music. Mom put in a tape with songs on it and we sang along. Our favorite song was one that went like this:

> LISSY: **There was a hole . . .**
> PACY & KI-KI : **There was a hole . . .**
> LISSY: **The prettiest hole . . .**
> PACY & KI-KI: **The prettiest hole . . .**
> LISSY: **That you ever did see . . .**
> PACY & KI-KI: **That you ever did see . . .**

The song kept going on like that, with a bird's nest in the tree that grew from the hole. We made Mom play it over and over again. Dad got very tired of the song. He said he was going to put the tape in a hole.

When we finally got to Albert's house it was dark

outside. But Auntie Kim, Uncle Leo, Grandma, and Grandpa and lots of other cousins, aunts, and uncles came out and welcomed us inside. They were all wearing their special silk clothes, and in the moonlight we shimmered like a stained-glass window. Grandma's dress was a silky, silver gray. She glowed liked a pearl ring. All our relatives hugged and kissed us and asked, "Ja-ba, bei?" over and over again. That meant, "Have you eaten yet?" in Taiwanese.

I thought that was a silly question. Of course, we hadn't eaten yet! We had all been in the car the whole time.

It was so crowded in the house. Red eggs were everywhere. Albert's name was written in Chinese on big pieces of red paper. Grandma and Grandpa hugged us again and again. We hadn't seen them in a long time. Cousin Jimmy, Sylvia, and Austin were there; so were Uncle Wally and Aunt Judy. So many people!

煮 鴨 內
WELCOME ALBERT!

Albert's Banner

Albert was sleeping in a crib. I don't know how he could sleep with all those people around, but he did.

He had a round, fat face with red cheeks. He looked like a red egg. But it could have been because he was sleeping on all those red envelopes. Relatives kept

Albert

coming by and slipping those envelopes stuffed with money into the crib. It reminded me that I still had to think about how I was going to get rich. Lucky Albert! He was already rich.

On the table there were brown stir-fried noodles; cooked duck shiny with oil; fresh lychees with their prickly pink skins; eggplant in brown sauce; shrimp with vegetables; snow-white rice; and puffy, white pork buns with flame-colored meat. There was also a big bowl of yellow ginger and chicken soup.

"Only women can eat that," Uncle Leo told us. "It gives them energy so they can take care of babies."

Since Lissy, and Ki-Ki, and I were girls, we decided to try a little. Besides, it was fun to be able to eat something the boys couldn't have. It was thick and oily tasting. We didn't really like it, but we pretended it was delicious—just to make Cousin Jimmy jealous.

While we were all at the table, Uncle Sam came downstairs to welcome us.

"Ja-ba, bei?" he asked us. "Have you eaten yet?"

They kept asking that. Grown-ups were so silly.

"We're eating RIGHT NOW!" I said.

Everyone laughed. I didn't understand why they were all laughing at me.

"What's so funny?" I demanded.

Mom explained to me that even though "Ja-ba, bei?" meant, "Have you eaten yet?" it was also a Taiwanese way of just saying, "How are you doing?"

"It's because food is so important to us," Uncle Leo told me. "Everything is about food."

"Yes," Auntie Kim said, and she pointed to Albert's name banner. "Do you know what Albert's name means? It means 'cooking duck'! See, we even name you kids after food."

"Really?" It was funny. I laughed with everyone else. "Then can I have some more Albert?"

Everyone laughed as Mom put more duck on my plate.

Chapter 11

Tiger Chasing Pig

slippers

THERE WERE A LOT OF PEOPLE STAYING AT ALBERT'S house. All the uncles and aunts tried to plan who should sleep where. It didn't seem like there would be enough room for all of us. Dad said they should make all the kids go sleep in the driveway. We didn't like that! Finally, Auntie Kim unrolled a bunch of sleeping bags and all the kids slept on the floor in the dining room. Lissy, Ki-Ki, Cousin Jimmy, and I slept underneath the table.

The next morning, when I opened my eyes, I saw a pair of gold embroidered slippers full of feet in front of my face. I sat up quickly and hit my head on the table.

"Ouch!" I said.

"Careful!" I heard Aunt Judy say. "You almost made the juice spill!"

I looked around and saw legs all around me, like prison bars. I heard glasses clinking and bowls moving overhead. I pushed through two pairs of legs and crawled out from under the table.

sleeping under the table

"Aren't you lucky?" Dad said. "You get to have breakfast in bed!"

"No, it's breakfast *over* bed!" Lissy said, and everyone laughed.

Mom got a chair for me and gave me a bowl of steaming rice porridge. She put some fried egg and my favorite—flaky, salty dried pork—on top of the bowl. As I bent my head to eat, I felt a sharp pain in my neck.

"My neck hurts!" I complained.

"Oh, probably from sleeping on the floor," Mom said. "It'll go away."

"Eh?" Grandma asked. Grandma and Grandpa didn't speak English that well, so sometimes they didn't know what we were talking about.

Mom spoke to Grandma in Taiwanese, repeating what I had said.

"Ah," Grandma nodded her head at me wisely, "I know. I fix!"

After breakfast Grandma brought me into her room. She took out a small green silk box that had dragons embroidered on it. Was Grandma going to give me a necklace? That was the only thing that I could imagine would be in such a special box.

But when she opened the box there was only a bamboo paintbrush, the color of dried grass, and some dull black stones inside. Grandma rubbed

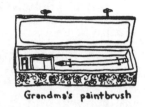

Grandma's paintbrush

the black stones with some water and I could see they were making a deep black ink. Grandma motioned me over, turned me around, and pushed the back of my shirt collar down. Then she had me hold up my hair.

"This is tiger," Grandma said, and I felt the cool tip of the paintbrush touch the back of my neck like a wet butterfly wing. She made some quick movements, and I felt the paintbrush flutter. "This is pig," she said.

Then Grandma blew a soft breeze on my neck to help the paint dry.

"Leave and tiger will chase pig," she told me. "Running will help neck."

What was she talking about? And what had she done? I went to the bathroom and stared. I had black marks, like leopard spots, painted on both sides of my neck. Would it wash off? I didn't dare do it right away; Grandma had said, "Leave." But what if my skin got stained black with those marks? And what was it that she was saying about pigs and tigers running?

I ran to show Mom. When she saw the paint, she laughed.

"She painted the Chinese symbol for tiger on one side of your neck and a pig on the other," she told me. "The tiger should chase the pig and the  running will massage your neck and make your neck feel better."

"Will the paint come off?" I asked. "I don't want to go to school with 'pig' written on my neck!"

"I'm sure it will," Mom said, "but does your neck feel better?"

I stopped and thought for a moment.

"Well, yeah," I nodded, "it does!"

Chapter 12

Luck

Melody's
notebook

THE PAINT DID WASH OFF AND SOON WE WERE hugging all our cousins and aunts and Grandma and Grandpa good-bye and driving home. When I went back to school, even though I had been gone for three whole days, nothing had changed. The only thing that was different was that I was behind on all my homework.

Melody was glad I was back. As soon as she saw me, she ran to tell me the news.

"Guess what?" Melody said. "Becky said that Heather said that Teddy likes someone."

She was talking about Teddy Jackson. We both had a crush on him. He had brown-blond hair, the color of sand, and blue eyes like a rainy sky. He was the cutest boy in the whole school. Or at least, I thought so; Melody thought Sam Mercer was cuter.

"Really!" I said. "Who?"

"She doesn't know," Melody said. "But she said it is someone who plays the violin."

"Then it could be one of us!" I almost shrieked.

Melody nodded vigorously with a big grin. Then she stopped. "But there are lots of other girls who play the violin."

I started to count—Emma Richards, Sophie Williams, Charlotte Fitzgerald, and then Melody and me. That was five girls. Which one of us did he like?

Melody and I became spies. We watched Teddy talk to every girl and studied him. Every time he walked into the room, we noted what he did, what he said, and who he spoke to. Melody wrote everything down in her notebook.

Melody as a spy

"Today, Teddy talked to Emma three times, Charlotte five times, you four times, and me six," Melody reported. "He picked up Charlotte's pencil, he held the door for you, and he let me cut in front of him in the lunch line."

"What about Sophie?" I asked.

"He never talks to Sophie," Melody said, "or even looks at her. It's definitely not her."

By Friday, Melody had filled her notebook. She

came over to my house for dinner and then we went over our Teddy notes. We had wonton soup (white, silky dumplings swimming in a bamboo-colored broth), stir-fried green cabbage, white rice, and sticky red-brown spareribs for dinner.

"I love spare ribs," I said as Mom cleared the plates from the table.

"I almost didn't make these tonight. You were going to get leftovers," Mom told us. "You're lucky!"

"We're supposed to be lucky," Melody told me as we went upstairs to my room. "We were both born in the Year of the Tiger, and tigers and dogs are friends. So the Year of the Dog is a lucky year for us."

"Do you think it'll be so lucky that Teddy Jackson likes one of us?" I asked, as we studied the notebook.

"It's either you or Charlotte," Melody said. "He smiles at both of you equally. He talked to her three more times then he did to you, but he did sit next to you in art class."

I thought about Charlotte. She had curly brown hair like a poodle and a freckled nose. She played violin better than I did.

"Maybe it's her," I said.

"But in art class, Teddy said his favorite color was black," Melody said, "and you have black hair."

Maybe it WAS me. A warm feeling started to bubble

up in me. Melody and I colored in a heart in her notebook.

"Teddy likes you! Teddy likes you!" Melody sang. "You're so lucky. Can I be a bridesmaid?"

wedding drawing

"Okay!" I said and we drew pictures of the wedding dress, the bridesmaids' dresses, and the cake.

That whole weekend, Melody called me "Mrs. Jackson." It was funny. Once, Mom answered the phone and said, "Sorry, you have the wrong number," and hung up on her. I had to call her back.

"Maybe Teddy will ask me to go out with him," I said to Melody. "Maybe he'll ask me to eat lunch with him!"

"Maybe," Melody said.

"Teddy and I could do a science fair project together!" I said.

"But *we* were going to do a science fair project together," Melody said, and suddenly she didn't sound so happy anymore.

"Well, all three of us can do it together, right?" I said.

"Maybe," Melody said again.

Then I remembered that Melody had liked Teddy, too. Maybe she felt bad because Teddy liked me and not her. Maybe she felt unlucky. I didn't realize that my good luck would be her bad luck. I didn't know what to do.

If Teddy became my boyfriend, what would I do? Would Melody be mad at me? Would we no longer be almost twins? I thought that maybe I shouldn't go out with Teddy. But he was so cute!

The next day at school, I met Melody on the playground.

"Is Teddy here yet?" I asked.

Melody shrugged. "I don't know."

For the first time since we met, Melody and I didn't know what to say to each other. Melody kicked small stones in the dirt and I watched them roll.

Becky came running up to us.

"Hey, did you hear," Becky said. "Teddy Jackson has a girlfriend!"

"He does?!" Melody and I said together.

"Yes," Becky said, "he and Sophie Williams are going out! He told her he liked her yesterday at the soccer game. Look!"

Melody and I looked at where Becky was pointing. We saw the back of Teddy and Sophie's heads, like two dandelions in the grass. They were holding hands.

Melody and I looked at each other and smiled.

Chapter 13

The Book Contest

my drawing

MY TWO FAVORITE CLASSES AT SCHOOL WERE library class and art class. At the library we were allowed to borrow three books at a time and Ms. McCurdy would read to us. I loved books. I read every Betsy book in the library. Then I read all the books by an author named Ruth Chew. Her books were all about magic and witches. They were so exciting.

I loved art class, too. Mr. Valente taught us how to mix colors. My favorite color was red, but you can't mix red. You can make orange from red and yellow or purple from red and blue, but you could never mix two colors together and get red. We also got to make pictures on scratchboard. Instead of drawing black lines on a white sheet of paper, you scratched away the black surface with a special pen. I did a drawing of some flowers against the moon.

One day, Ms. McCurdy came to our art class. It was funny seeing her there because we usually only saw her in the library.

"Hello, class," she said, "Mr. Valente and I are combining our classes for a very special project. We are going to have all of you write and illustrate your own books!"

Our own books? Could we do that? Could I do that?

Ms. McCurdy told us there was a contest that we would be entering. It was called "Written and Illustrated by . . . The National Awards Contest for Students." For this contest, you entered books that you wrote and drew yourself. If you won first place, they would publish your book, just like the books in the library. Ms. McCurdy would help us with the writing, and Mr. Valente would help us with the drawing. But we had to think up our own ideas.

All day long, I thought about the project. Becky said she was going to do her book about a unicorn. Melody said she might write a story about a singer. I heard some boys talk about how they were going to do their stories about pirates or wizards with swords. I couldn't decide what to do mine about.

At home, I told everyone about the project.

"Do a book about a girl that can read minds," Lissy said.

"Do something with panda bears," Ki-Ki said.

"How about a cookbook?" Mom said.

"Better make it an eating book," Dad said. "You're good at that."

"No," I said, "those aren't good ideas. I need a good idea so I can win the contest."

Mom shook her head. "It's not easy to win a contest. You have to work very hard."

"Yes," said Dad, "like how you practice the violin. Everything takes time and effort."

"So, I have to practice making a book every day?" I asked. "That doesn't make any sense."

"No," Mom said, "but you'll have to work on your book a little bit every day, if you want it to be good. Just like practicing an instrument. Did I ever tell you about Grandma and the paper piano?"

THE PAPER PIANO

When I was a little girl, maybe a little bit younger than you are, before Grandpa started his business, we were very poor. Our house was small and old with a cracked cement floor that was never clean, no matter how much Grandma swept and scrubbed it. The bathroom was broken down and rotten, green mold grew underneath the sink, and when it rained, worms would come out of the walls.

Grandma didn't like being poor. Before she married Grandpa, she had been a fine lady. Now, we were the poor family of a medical student. But Grandma knew it was only temporary. Once Grandpa became established, we would live in a nice house and I would grow up to be a fine lady, just like she had been. So while we were waiting for Grandpa to get established, she wanted me to learn all the things fine ladies knew. And one of those things was how to play the piano.

Grandma looked all over for a good piano teacher that we could afford. Finally, she found one. He was a young man who lived over a mile away. Since we were too poor to buy a piano, he said that I could come to his house to practice every day after he was done giving lessons.

the piano teacher's house

Every day, I walked the long way to his house. He lived in a grand house. I used to think that it was probably just like the house Elvis Presley would live in because it was an American-style house. Outside the house was a garden with a rainbow of flowers. There were exotic flowers in the garden—red and yellow roses with their vivid petals spilling over each other, marigolds looking like bursts of orange sunshine, and brilliant violet pink petunias. The house, itself, had two floors. I never got to see what was upstairs, but the downstairs was so magnificent! The floor was smooth and glossy wood, polished like a piece of golden amber. There were curly carved tea chests and furniture, shiny chestnut-colored striped curtains, and ivory glass vases with blue flowers painted on them. On the porcelain cover of a gold box, an English lady smiled at me. She wore a big pink dress, the skirts puffing like an upside-down peony. She always seemed to be inviting me to open the box, but I never dared. The paintings of wealthy ancestors were watching. Their stern gazes forbade me to touch any of their riches. My piano teacher had a fascinating house.

the gold box

But the walk to his house was long and dull. By the time I got there, my legs ached as if they had been beaten with bamboo stalks. I always tried to get out of going to his house. "It's too hot," I would say, or "It's raining." But no matter what I said, Grandma still would make me go practice. Every day she marched me out of the house. Until, finally one day, she grew tired of hearing me complain. "Okay," she said. "You don't have to go. But you still have to practice."

I was confused. If I didn't have to go, how would I practice? How could I practice without a piano?

But Grandma calmly took out a big sheet of paper. She cut it and measured it and colored it in. It was only after she had filled in all the black rectangles that I recognized what she had made. It was a drawing of a piano keyboard.

Grandma put the paper piano and my music on the table in front of me and said, "Here, you can practice on this."

I played my scales, my exercises, and my solo. Every time I touched a paper key, Grandma would sing the note.

Mom (as a little girl),
Grandma, and
the paper piano

"So, no matter what, I practiced the piano every day. Sometimes I practiced on a real piano; sometimes I practiced on the paper piano. It was a long time before we got a piano of our own, but when we did, I was able to play so well that they invited me to play in the school orchestra. Later, I played a solo at a big concert and when I was done everyone stood up and clapped. Grandma was so happy that she cried," Mom finished.

"So if I win the book contest, will you cry?" I asked.

"Yes," Mom said. "Very hard."

"We'll all cry," Dad said. "I'll buy a box of Kleenex just for the occasion."

Chapter 14

Trying to Discover

ice cream

BESIDES THE BOOK PROJECT, THE OTHER EXCITING thing going on at school was the science fair. Since Teddy Jackson wasn't going to be my boyfriend, Melody and I were partners, just like we planned. I couldn't wait for the science fair. I thought, maybe, it could help me find myself. If science could answer questions about the weather and nature, it had to be able to help answer what I was going to be when I grew up.

"Becky and Charlotte are doing a project on constellations," I said to Melody. "And Teddy and Sophie are making a volcano. What are we going to do?"

Teddy and Sophie's volcano

"I don't know," she said, "but let's do something that'll win the blue ribbon. I've never won one before."

"Me neither," I said. "We'd have to be really lucky to win the blue ribbon, though."

"But we're supposed to be lucky this year," Melody said. "We should be able to get it."

Mom overheard us.

"The science fair isn't about luck," she told us. "It's about science. Discovery through using your senses—sight, smell, sound, touch, and taste."

"Taste?" I said. "Let's do a project about ice cream. I can discover ice cream."

"That's not science," Melody said, "that's dessert!"

Mom tried to help us. "You should do an experiment, something you don't know the answer to before you begin," she said.

"Like what?" I asked. Mom knew about these things because she used to be a plant scientist before she married Dad. A botanist, she said.

"Well," Mom said, "a famous scientist once had her plants listen to different kinds of music to see if it would affect their growth. She put a plant in a room and played classical music in the room twenty-four hours a day. In another room, she played rock music."

"Did it make a difference?" Melody asked.

"Yes, it did," Mom told us. "The plant that listened to classical music grew more than the one that listened to rock music."

"That's funny!" I laughed. "Plants don't like rock music!"

"Hmm," Melody said, "maybe we should do something like that."

"I don't want to have music playing all the time!" I said. "I'll never get to sleep."

"Maybe we can do something else, like using different colored lights or water," Melody said.

"I know!" I said. "We can water the plants with different things! We'll give one orange juice, another soda, and one milk, and see which one they like better."

Melody laughed. "Maybe we should feed one ice cream, too!"

So, that weekend we planted four pea plant seeds. We watered one with orange juice, one with milk, one with ginger ale, and one with plain water. Mom called that one our "control"; we compared the others to it.

The plants didn't grow very well. The milk plant had one shriveled stem and smelled funny. The orange juice plant was just a pot of dirt. The water plant was small. In fact, the only plant that looked good was the plant we fed ginger ale. It was strong and green with a vine climbing up the stick.

soda plant

"Plants like soda!" Melody announced. "We should tell the world! Everyone should water their plants with soda from now on. People could hose their lawns with ginger ale!"

Melody and I made big posters for the science fair. We made charts of each plant and wrote a report. The report was four pages long. I drew a leaf border on every page. We were very proud.

"This is our lucky year," Melody told me. "We're definitely going to win the blue ribbon. And after the science fair hears about our project, we'll be famous! Maybe we'll be in the newspapers or on TV."

I was excited, too. Not only had Melody and I made an important scientific discovery, I might have discovered my talent. I could be a scientist! I could be like Albert Einstein, but I would comb my hair.

"Do you think the pea from the soda plant will taste like ginger ale?" Melody asked.

We looked at the plant. It didn't look like any peas were growing.

"Maybe it'll grow a pea pod by the science fair," I said hopefully.

Chapter 15

The **Science Fair**

blue ribbon

THE SCIENCE FAIR WAS ON SATURDAY. IT DIDN'T seem fair that we had to go to school on a Saturday, but our teachers said it was the only way everyone could see all the projects. I was glad everyone was going to see our project; I couldn't wait until they heard what we discovered.

Feed Your Plant Soda for Optimal Growth by Melody Ling and Grace Lin

our science fair banner

Melody and I taped our posters on the wall. Our largest poster said "Feed Your Plant Soda for Optimal Growth." I had drawn a picture of a pea plant and a bottle of ginger ale next to it. We hung that one right in the middle. We put our plants on the table with a carton of milk, a bottle of soda, a cup of orange juice, and a watering can. The plants were very small and scrawny—they didn't look anything like my drawings.

Becky and Charlotte came over to our table while I was trying to make our plants look better by drawing pic-  tures on the pots. The pictures didn't help.

our science fair plants

"Those plants don't look that good," Charlotte said. "Did you really water one with soda?"

"Yes!" Melody said. "And we made a scientific discovery! This our lucky year!"

Becky and Charlotte looked puzzled, so I explained the idea to them.

"Melody and I were born in the Year of the Tiger," I told them, "so the Year of the Dog is really lucky for us. We'll probably win the blue ribbon."

"But I'm the same age as you," Becky said, "so I was born in the Year of the Tiger, too. So, that means I'm just as lucky as you are. Maybe we'll win the blue ribbon."

Melody and I looked at each other. We hadn't thought of that. How could all of us be lucky when there was only one blue ribbon?

"We're luckier because it's the Chinese Year of the Dog," Melody said, "and Grace and I are Chinese."

I could see Becky didn't agree, but Ms. Malone

(Melody's teacher) came into the room and told everyone to go stand by their projects.

"We're ready to start judging the science fair," Ms. Malone said. "And this year we are especially lucky! My good friend Mr. McKnealy is going to be our guest judge. He is a scientist. He works at NASA."

"Lucky!" Melody nudged me. "See! With him here, we'll definitely get the blue ribbon."

"But he's from NASA!" I whispered to Melody. "That's like the space shuttle! He's probably an astronaut; he won't know about plants."

"Astronauts are scientists," she whispered back, "and scientists know about science. We're going to win. I know it!"

We waited a long time for Mr. McKnealy to come to our project. When he did, he looked surprised.

"Well, this is an interesting project," he said, and he picked up our report and started reading it.

We nudged each other. Here was our good luck!

"However," he said to us, "I'm not sure your results substantiate your claim. Were your plants in a controlled environment?"

I looked at Melody. Her grin had completely disappeared.

"Our water plant is the control," I told him, remembering what Mom had called it. I felt very smart.

"No, I meant did you give each plant the same amount of liquid and did they each get the same sun exposure?" he said.

"Well, there wasn't enough room in the window for the water plant so I put that one on the table in the other room," I said, suddenly not feeling very smart. "It might have gotten less light. And we didn't measure how much we gave them."

"Hmm," Mr. McKnealy said, frowning, "then I'm afraid your scientific method was seriously flawed."

Melody and I looked at each other. We didn't feel so lucky anymore.

"To get true results, you should do this project over again with at least ten plants for each liquid, in a controlled environment." He continued, "And then you should do a chlorophyll test. . . ."

When he left, Melody and I were very quiet.

"I don't think he liked it," Melody said.

"He did say it was interesting," I said.

"But, I really thought we had discovered something," Melody said. She sounded glum. "He thought it was a terrible project."

"He didn't say it was terrible," I said.

"He said we were seriously flawed!" Melody said. "That's scientist talk for terrible!"

We sat down at our table, depressed. The science

fair that had been so colorful and thrilling an hour ago was now grey and dull.

"I didn't know scientists had to do all of that stuff," I said. Maybe I didn't want to be a scientist after all. It looked like I didn't have any science talent. "Did you know what he was talking about?"

"No!" Melody said and we both laughed.

An hour later, Ms. Malone came back into the room. We watched her hand Charlotte and Becky the blue ribbon. Then their pictures were taken for the school newspaper.

"I guess Charlotte and Becky have more luck than we do after all," Melody said, "even though they're not Chinese."

"Maybe because Becky has a dog," I said. "Dogs are probably better friends with other dogs than they are with tigers."

"Yeah," Melody said, "Scruffy probably put in a good word for them."

"Or maybe they just had a better project," I said.

"Maybe," Melody said, "but I bet it was Scruffy."

Scruffy

Chapter 16

Dreaming of Dorothy

my drawings

WE KNEW THE END OF THE SCHOOL YEAR WAS
coming when Ms. Malone announced that there were
sign-ups for the school play.

"This year," she told our grade, "we are going to put
on the musical play *The Wizard of Oz*. You can choose
to be in the orchestra or the choir, or you can try out
for one of the parts."

The Wizard of Oz! I loved the movie and the book.
Right away, I knew I was going to try out for Dorothy.
Since it looked like I wasn't going to be a scientist
when I grew up, I wouldn't mind being a rich movie
star. This could be my chance to see if I had talent as
an actress.

Melody and I looked at the sign-up sheet.

"I'm signing up for the orchestra," Melody told me.

"You're not going to try out for Dorothy?" I said. "I am!"

"I'm not going to sing in front of all those people," Melody said, looking at the list. "Besides, everyone wants to be Dorothy."

That was true. The list for Dorothy was very long. Almost all the girls in our grade had signed up. I made the list even longer.

That whole week I practiced being Dorothy. In class, I drew pictures of Dorothy in her checkered dress. At home I drew Dorothy's ruby shoes while I sang "Somewhere Over the Rainbow." I practiced singing every day—after school, after dinner, in the bathroom, and before bed.

"Why can't you sing 'Somewhere. . . ' elsewhere?" Lissy groaned. "Anywhere but here!"

I wasn't the only one singing, though. On the day of the audition it seemed like every girl was singing. You could hear "Somewhere Over the Rainbow" on the bus, in the girl's bathroom, and on the playground.

"I'm going to play on the swings," Melody said, covering her ears. "I'm sick of that song."

I kept singing with the other girls. We all crowded together like a flock of excited crows. Even while we

69

sang, all of us were wondering the same thing. Who would get the part? Who was going to be Dorothy? The thought was thrilling and delicious at the same time.

"Do you think I could be Dorothy?" I asked Becky.

Becky looked at me in shock.

"You can't be Dorothy," she said. "Dorothy's not Chinese."

Suddenly, the world went silent. Like a melting icicle, my dream of being Dorothy fell and shattered on the ground. I felt like a dirty puddle after the rain. All the girls continued singing, but I didn't hear them. Becky was right. Dorothy wasn't Chinese. I was SO dumb. How could I have even thought about being Dorothy? I'd never get chosen. It was stupid to even try.

When Ms. Malone called my name at the audition, I shook my head.

"Are you sure?" she asked.

I nodded and Ms. Malone called on the next girl.

The next day, a list was posted with all the parts. I was a munchkin and Emma Richards was Dorothy. Emma had brown hair that curled at the ends and blue eyes. When she wore the blue-check- ered dress, she'd look just like Dorothy.

Emma as Dorothy

"How come Chinese people are never important?" I asked Melody.

"What do you mean?" she said. "We're important."

"No, we're not," I said. "You never see a Chinese person in the movies or in a play or in a book. No one Chinese is important."

"There are Chinese movie stars," Melody said, "and the woman that does the news in Chinese."

"Not a lot, though," I said. "And there are none in books. Whenever we do a school play, it's always from books and none of the characters are Chinese. We did Cinderella, Peter Pan, Alice in Wonderland—nobody in books is Chinese."

"There must be," Melody said. "Just because the school hasn't done a play about a Chinese person doesn't mean there aren't any."

"I doubt it," I said. "I bet there aren't any."

Melody and I went to the library and asked for a Chinese book. We looked at the book *The Five Chinese Brothers.*

a Chinese book

"See," Melody said, "Chinese people."

"Those aren't real Chinese people, though," I said. "Your brother doesn't have a ponytail."

"It's not supposed to be real," Melody said. "Who can swallow the ocean like they do in the book?"

"But I wanted a real Chinese person book," I complained. "One with people like us—Chinese-Americans."

"You're just being picky," Melody said. "Go write your own, then."

"Okay," I said, suddenly remembering the book contest. "I will."

Chapter 17

A Real Chinese Person Book

my dog doodle

MAKING A BOOK WAS A LOT HARDER THAN SAYING I would make one. When I told Ms. McCurdy that I wanted to make a book with a Chinese-American person in it she was very excited.

"That's a wonderful idea," she told me. "Why don't you write about yourself? You're a Chinese-American, and if you write your own experiences, your book is sure to be very unique."

Ms. McCurdy said over and over again that she wanted us to make books with unique and original ideas. She always tried to make us write stories from our own lives. "Write what you know!" she kept telling us. But most of us didn't seem to know much because we weren't doing very original ideas. Charlotte wrote a story that sounded a lot like Cinderella, except instead of two stepsisters there was only one. Becky's story was a lot like the unicorn movie we watched.

Melody's Book

Melody was doing an original idea, though. Her book was about flowers that talked to each other. She got the idea from our science fair project. She said since she learned plants had tastes like people, she'd write a story about them talking like people, too.

But even with an original idea, I still didn't know what to write about. I knew I wanted it to be about a Chinese person and Ms. McCurdy wanted me to write about my life, but I couldn't think of a part of my life to write about. There was just nothing exciting in my life. Maybe that was why there were no real Chinese people in books; we all had boring lives.

I watched the rest of the class write their stories. I drew little pictures of dogs reading books. My mind was like an empty paper balloon.

Ms. McCurdy stopped by my desk. "Writer's block?" she asked me.

"What's writer's block?" I asked.

"It's when a writer can't think of what to write about, when you can't think of any words to write," she told me.

I nodded my head hard. I definitely was having writer's block!

"What's the cure for it?" I asked.

"You just have to relax, not try so hard," Ms. McCurdy said, "and wait."

Well, that was disappointing. "Isn't there something I could do to make it disappear sooner?" I asked her.

"Don't worry," Ms. McCurdy told me. "You'll find an idea. It will come to you."

But I worried. Finding a book idea was like finding myself. And I wasn't having much luck with either!

Chapter 18

The School Play

singing tryouts

AT THE SAME TIME AS THE BOOK PROJECT, WE were also working on *The Wizard of Oz*. There were rehearsals every week. Since I was only a munchkin, I thought rehearsals were pretty boring.

"I should've signed up for the orchestra, like you," I told Melody. "Who ever heard of a Chinese munchkin?"

"That's not why I signed up for the orchestra," Melody said. "Besides, no one will see you, probably."

"That's true," I said, thinking about all the kids that were munchkins on stage. All we did was stand around and sing songs.

But one day, Ms. Malone said, "Right before the song, we need a munchkin to give Dorothy a thank-you gift for killing the Wicked Witch. Grace, we'll have you do it."

Me! But then everyone would see me! What if I handed Dorothy the gift and everyone in the audience whispered to each other, "A Chinese munchkin? There's no such thing as a Chinese munchkin!"

I tried to say something, but Ms. Malone had hurried on to the Cowardly Lion.

That day when I got home from school, Mom asked me what was wrong.

"Uh-oh," Mom said, "you have a grumpy face. What's wrong today?"

"Miss Malone made me the munchkin that gives Dorothy the gift," I said.

"Isn't that good?" Mom asked. "Now you have a part that's more special."

"No," I told her. "It's horrible. It's so stupid that she picked me."

"Why is it stupid?" Mom asked. "I would think you'd be proud."

"Now everyone will see me!" I said. "Before, no one would notice me, but now I'll stick out. People will say, 'Grace is a munchkin?' and then they'll laugh at me. Everyone is going to laugh at me!"

"Hmm," Mom said. "You sound like I did before my first day of school. Did I ever tell you about that?"

The night before my first day of school, my mother told me that Amah, my grandmother, was going to bring me. Now, remember, Amah grew up during a time when women bound their feet to make them smaller. Binding their feet did make them smaller, but oh, how painful it was to walk on them! So, because it was so difficult for Amah to walk, it was decided that Amah would walk me to school and wait outside for me all day until it was time to bring me back so she wouldn't have to make an extra trip.

Now, was I grateful for Amah's sacrifice? No! I was embarrassed. What would my classmates think of me when my grandmother walked me to school and sat all day in the schoolyard waiting for me? They would think I was a baby who needed someone nearby all the time. I pleaded and begged for my parents to let me go alone or for someone else to bring me. But they refused.

The next day, I dreaded going to school. Usually I liked walking with Amah. Unlike walking with my mother or father, whose large steps made me hop like a rabbit, Amah always walked slowly and deliberately, picking her steps like the way you choose peaches at the market. But today,

Mom (as a little girl) walking to school

I hated walking with Amah. I dragged my feet as if they were stuck to the ground with honey. I hoped that by getting to school late, no one would see Amah walking with me.

On the way, we met up with another student, a round-faced boy named Xiao-Jay, who was walking with his grandmother as well. He scowled at me with fierce anger and I started to feel that school was going to be a very unhappy and unfriendly place.

The bell was ringing when we finally reached the school. So far, my plan was working. I hoped that no one noticed Amah as I left her outside. But my relief was short-lived because as soon as my classmates sat down in their seats, Xiao-Jay made a noise like a teakettle. 'Look out the window!' he laughed and pointed.

I was horrified. Was this terrible boy pointing at Amah and laughing at her? I joined my classmates at the window, and then I started laughing, too.

Outside, in the schoolyard, sat a whole row of grandmothers!

Row of Grandmothers

"They sat there like a line of birds on a telephone wire, gossiping and sharing tea. Everyone's grandmother was out there. I didn't need to feel embarrassed about Amah waiting for me the whole day," Mom finished, "because everyone else's grandmother was doing the same thing."

"But it's not the same with the play," I said.

"Isn't it, though?" Mom asked. "You're so worried about your part, you aren't seeing that there is nothing to worry about."

"Maybe," I said, but I did feel better.

Chapter 19

The **Wizard** of **Oz**

my gift to
Dorothy

ON THE NIGHT OF THE SCHOOL PLAY, THE SKY
was as quiet as a feather falling. It was still and silent
without movement from the wind or snow. I couldn't
understand it at all. How could it be so calm when the
play was about to happen?

Backstage, everyone was running around, getting
dressed and putting on makeup. Tin cans were being
polished, straw was taped on, and green backdrops
were whizzing around. Cathy Small, who played
Glinda, had gotten her hair permed just for the
occasion.

I didn't have much to do. I had already put on my
flowered munchkin apron and bonnet. Even though I
didn't look like a munchkin, my costume was perfect.
Most of the munchkins had used old clothes belong-
ing to their parents or grandparents to make their

costumes, but my parents didn't have anything that looked right. So Mom and I went to the store and I picked out a leaf-green material with delicate rosebuds scattered on it. It was called calico, which was what the American pioneer girls wore, and it was exactly right for a munchkin.

me as a munchkin

I also had my gift that I was supposed to hand to Dorothy. It was a shoe box covered with sapphire blue wrapping paper and a big red bow. It was completely empty. I could toss it in the air like a balloon. But that didn't matter because Dorothy never ended up opening it—which I didn't think was right. If I were given a gift from a munchkin, I'd open it right away.

Melody and I watched everyone rush around. It was as if there were a hurricane happening all around us.

"This is why I didn't try out to be Dorothy," Melody told me. "Too stressful!"

"True," I said, "but it's exciting, too. When you're one of us, without an important role, it's pretty boring."

"You've got an important role," Melody said. "You're the gift-giving munchkin!"

"Yeah, I'm giving an empty box," I said. "Great present!"

"Actually, Danny Dog has the biggest role out of all

of us," Melody laughed. Danny Dog was Melody's stuffed animal. He was going to be Toto. Becky had volunteered Scruffy, but Ms. Malone said a real dog would be "unreliable," so Melody brought fuzzy, chocolate-colored Danny

Danny Dog

Dog. Most of the time, Danny Dog was carried in Dorothy's basket, so he didn't really get to do much either—though one of the boys did bark offstage to give him a voice.

Melody was dressed all in black. All the orchestra was dressed in black so they wouldn't be too obvious. Melody wanted to wear black makeup, too, but Ms. Malone said it wouldn't be necessary.

"Grace, Melody," Ms. Malone said. "Get to your places. The curtains will go up in ten minutes."

Melody waved good-bye as she went to the orchestra pit, which was the area in front of the stage. I joined the other munchkins and thought about the play.

First, Emma would be in her blue-checkered Dorothy costume (which was made from a tablecloth) talking to Toto (Danny Dog) and then the curtains would open and show Oz. Then the munchkins would come and sing and then I would give the gift. I knew Mom was right and probably everyone was too busy thinking about their own parts to wonder why there was a Chinese munchkin, but I was still worried. Would they laugh and whisper?

I heard clapping from the audience. It was loud. That meant there were probably a lot of people! I tried to smooth out the wrinkled wrapping paper on my gift.

Ms. Malone beckoned us and all the munchkins filed through the door and went onstage.

Never before did the stage feel so big. I was glad there were other munchkins in front and in back of me. Emma looked so much like Dorothy with her braided hair and blue and white dress that I forgot for a second that I was in a play, and I thought I was watching her on TV. The orchestra played and the munchkins began to sing. As soon as the song was over, it would be time for ME. I opened and closed my mouth, but no words came out. I just looked at the space between Dorothy and me. How many steps would it be? Ten? Fourteen?

Suddenly, one of the munchkins nudged me.

"Grace!" the munchkin hissed. "Go!"

It was time! I walked forward, and there was a bright spotlight on me. I tried to look into the audience, but I couldn't see anyone. I didn't hear anything except for my own breathing. With every step I got closer to Emma and she smiled at me, a play smile full of teeth—one for the audience. As she took the gift, I felt like I was giving her a ten-pound rice sack. I curtsied like we had practiced, and as I looked at my shoes I heard thunder. It was applause! For me! No one had laughed or whispered about a Chinese munchkin at all! I smiled into the bright light toward the audience as I headed back to join the rest of the munchkins.

The rest of the play floated by like a soap bubble. Once I looked down at the orchestra pit and saw Melody making faces at me. I didn't dare make one back at her, but I couldn't help laughing. I pulled my bonnet over my face so no one could see.

After Dorothy clicked her heels three times and the play was over, everyone lined up for a bow. The audience gave us a standing ovation! That meant we must have been really good. I bet I had been the best gift-giving Chinese munchkin ever!

Wizard of Oz curtain call

Chapter 20

Digging Up a Book Idea

shovel

WHEN THE PLAY WAS OVER, EVERYONE WAS concentrating on the book project. Almost everyone had finished writing his or her stories and I hadn't even thought of a good idea. I still had writer's block! I knew Ms. McCurdy said an idea would come to me, but I didn't want to get a bad grade on the project because of writer's block. But I couldn't think of anything unique about me. I thought about writing about the science fair, like Melody, but since we didn't discover anything it didn't seem like it was a good idea. I thought about writing about Albert's Red Egg party, but that was about Albert, not me.

When I got home from school that day, I found Mom in the backyard. Spring was here; the snow had melted away for good and had left everything smelling like a wet towel. The leaves on the trees were just starting to peek out, looking like small emerald ornaments hanging on the branches, and my shoes were coated with mud, as if they had been dipped in chocolate. It was gardening time.

"Uh-oh," Mom said. "Grumpy face again. Did something go wrong at school?"

"I have writer's block," I told her. "I can't think of an idea to write for my book project. Everyone else is almost done writing their stories and I haven't even started."

"Hmm," Mom said. "Maybe if you help me dig, it'll loosen up your writer's block and give you an idea."

"That won't give me an idea!" I laughed. "You just want me to help you!"

Still, I put on my blue garden overalls and helped Mom dig anyway. Mom always needed help with her garden. It was because she grew special Chinese vegetables. It took a lot of time. We would dig and dig and then plant seeds that looked like medicine pills. After that we would water the whole garden with a hose so much that it looked as if there had been a flood.

Chinese vegetable seeds

While we were digging, Mom tried to help me come up with ideas.

"Why don't you write about the school play?" she suggested. "Or Chinese New Year?"

I kept shaking my head. None of the ideas seemed right. I threw the ideas away like we threw the dirt from our shovels. Soon we were both tired and decided to take a rest.

"I don't know if I'm more tired from digging dirt or digging for an idea for you," Mom said. "Digging is hard work."

"If you planted flowers instead of Chinese vegetables," I told her, "we wouldn't have to work so hard."

"But then you wouldn't get to eat your favorite soup," Mom told me. "Do you remember the first time I planted Chinese vegetables?"

I remembered. Mom's whole garden had been full of weird-looking Chinese vegetables—they were yellow and bumpy and lumpy. Some of them looked like warty frogs and some looked like purple sausages. I couldn't understand why she wanted to grow them. But when she made soup out of them, I changed my mind. The soup was SO good; eating it was like swallowing a nice warm hug after being in the cold.

Mom's soup

"You thought they were ugly vegetables," Mom laughed.

"They still are ugly," I told her, "but they taste delicious. Yummy ugly vegetables!"

Suddenly it hit me. Here was a good idea for my

book. I could write about the ugly vegetables and me!

"You were right," I told Mom. "Digging cured my writer's block!"

"Good," she said. "Now just imagine what will happen when you help me water."

an ugly
vegetable

Chapter 21

Making a Book

shelf of books

NOW THAT I HAD MY BOOK IDEA, I HAD TO WRITE the story. This wasn't easy. It took me all night to write the story. And that was just the first time. Mom read it and made me change things. Then Dad read it and made me change things. Lissy read it and told me to change everything, but I didn't listen to her. Finally, I read it to Ki-Ki and Melody and they said it was perfect. So, I brought it to school. Ms. McCurdy read it and liked it very much. But she made me change things, too. So I had to write my story over three times! Then, I had to type it all out. Mom helped me, but it still took a long time.

After the story was done, I drew and painted picture after picture. It was fun painting and drawing. I used all my favorite colors like rose violet and vermilion red. I made the vegetables look even uglier

my drawing of
an ugly vegetable

than they were in real life . . . and I made myself look prettier by making my eyelashes longer and always wearing a long, beautiful dress. I looked like a princess!

drawing of me
in my book

But, it was easy to make mistakes. Sometimes I would have to paint a picture two or three times before it was perfect. I never knew it was so hard to make a book! I even ran out of paint. Dad went out and bought me some new ones.

"The man at the store said these paints were not for beginners," Dad told me, "and I told him, 'My daughter is not a beginner!'"

I pasted the pictures and my story onto the pages. Ms. McCurdy and Mr. Valente helped me bind the book. I was so proud. If I won the contest, I couldn't imagine what they would do to it to make it more like a real book.

Before we sent the books to the contest, Ms. McCurdy showed each book to the class. I was embarrassed when she showed mine. I probably shouldn't have tried to make myself look prettier; it was kind of silly to garden in a long dress! I hoped they'd let me change that if it was ever printed as a real book.

Ms. McCurdy put all the books in the library on a special shelf she saved for us. She put them alphabetically by author, just like they did with real books. Mine was right next to Melody's.

Ms. McCurdy said we wouldn't hear from the contest until next year. She warned all of us not to hope too hard about winning the contest. She said it was a contest that everyone in the whole country would be entering, so it would be difficult to win. But, she also said, we should be proud of our books because they were all good and deserved to win a prize.

Next year was a long time to wait, I thought. But if they had to read the books of everyone in the whole country, I guess it made sense. Ms. McCurdy gave us our grades. I got an A+!

Melody came over to my house after school. She got an A on her book, too.

"Good job!" Mom said when we told her the news. "I know you both worked very hard on that project."

Mom sliced some red bean paste candy for us to snack on as a reward. The mahogany-colored candy was soft and sweet and coated our mouths.

red bean paste
jelly candy

"Did Ms. McCurdy say anything about your books besides your grade?" Mom asked.

"She said mine was beautiful," I said, nodding my head.

"Mine was 'Wonderfully unique,'" Melody said.

"Whose book did you like the best?" Mom asked.

"Sam Mercer's," Melody said, giving me a nudge. Now that Teddy had a girlfriend, we both liked Sam. "His book was all about a knight who killed people."

"That doesn't sound like a nice book," Mom said.

"No," we said in unison, "it was great!"

Chapter 22

No More School!

almond cookies

AFTER THE BOOK PROJECT WAS OVER, THE DAYS disappeared like dumplings on a plate. The sun shone with the yellow of summer and the wind blew a breeze that felt like it came from an oven. Almost before I knew it, the last bell was ringing and Melody and I were running to my house to celebrate the end of the school year.

Mom took out some crumbly almond cookies for us. Melody loved eating at my house. We had lots of food that was not nutritious.

"What is your family doing this summer?" Mom asked Melody.

"We're going to TAC camp again," she told us, "and then we're visiting my Aunt Alice in New Jersey."

"What's TAC camp?" I asked.

"Oh, it's a camp for Taiwanese-Americans. We all

get together and do things," she told me. "We go every summer. We spend a week there and then we go see my Aunt Alice the next week."

"That sounds boring," I said.

"No, it's fun!" Melody said. "We sing songs and go to art class—all the usual fun camp things, except everyone is Taiwanese. Maybe you should come!"

"But I can't speak Taiwanese like you," I said.

"That's okay," Melody said. "Everyone knows English; some of them don't know how to speak Taiwanese either. Anyway, I can help you. You should come, too! It would be fun!"

"Maybe she will," Mom said. "I think it would be good for Pacy to make more Taiwanese friends. I'm going to call your mother about this camp."

Mom found out more about the TAC camp. Melody's mother explained to her that it was really a Taiwanese-American Convention, which was kind of like a camp but it was for the whole family, not just kids. The adults would meet other Taiwanese-American parents and listen to speeches and things. The kids would get together and do crafts and watch movies. Mom thought it sounded good not just for me, but for the whole family, so we all drove down to the convention.

The first week of the convention was fun. Melody and I spent most of our time together. Sometimes we'd get bright-colored Popsicles in the shape of rockets and eat them, turning our mouths as purple as the pansies decorating the stairs we liked to

eating Popsicles

sit on. Sometimes we drew ice cream–colored chalk pictures of dogs or hearts (with our names and Sam Mercer's in them) or unicorns on the faded playground pavement. Once we held a stuffed animal wedding with Ki-Ki and Benji—Danny Dog married Sabrina (Benji's toy cat), and Butterscotch (my teddy

Butterscotch,
my teddy bear

bear) was the minister. It was a lovely wedding. Ki-Ki's pony toys carried away the bride and the groom. Lissy spent all her time with the big girls, dancing and shopping.

But after the first week, Melody's family had to leave. They were going to see her Aunt Alice in New Jersey. I was sad she was leaving.

"It's not going to be any fun now," I told her.

"Well, I'd rather stay here with you," Melody told me. "My Aunt Alice is strange."

"What do you mean strange?" I asked. "Does she have purple hair?"

"No," Melody said, "she looks normal. But she believes in ghosts. Did I tell you that the last time I visited her, I sat on a ghost?"

"What?" I asked. "How could you sit on a ghost?"

How Melody Sat on a Ghost

The last time we went to my Aunt Alice's, she invited us over for dinner. I think it was for Chinese New Year. I can't remember. Anyway, there were two chairs at the end of the table that were empty. Even though no one was sitting in the chairs, there were big plates of food there. I could smell the stir-fried noodles, the shiny roasted duck, and dragon red pork—they seemed to invite me over. So I sat down in one of the empty chairs, ready to eat.

Aunt Alice rushed over like a typhoon and hurried me out of the chair. She told me those chairs were for the ghosts of her parents. I thought she was joking, but she wasn't. She poured hot tea in two fancy cups and served them to the empty chairs. When she finished, she bowed with deep respect, her nose almost touching her knees.

It made me think, maybe there were ghosts there. Do you think they minded

special tea set

that I sat on them? I wonder if I sat on her father or her mother. But then again, maybe they weren't sitting down yet. I couldn't tell. I kept watching the chair cushions to see if they got wrinkled or anything when the ghosts sat down or stood up, but not one gold thread of embroidery moved.

My parents told me it was a way of honoring the dead. I was worried that the whole dinner was going to be for the ghosts and we weren't going to eat anything, but my mother told me we would get to eat after the ghosts were done. Then I was worried, because how would we know when the ghosts were done eating? I didn't see any food disappearing. We could be waiting a long time and the food would be cold.

But Aunt Alice seemed to know. She served all the courses, one by one, to the ghosts. After the last course was served, she took all the food back in the kitchen and reheated it. Then we got to eat.

"I sat next to one of the ghosts for the whole meal. At least I think I did. Maybe they moved around," Melody finished, "but they were pretty nice, as far as ghosts go."

"Do you know what that means?" I said. "You ate ghost leftovers!"

"Mmm," Melody said, "and they were delicious."

Chapter 23

A Twinkie

broken crayon

MOM SAID IT WAS GOOD MELODY WAS LEAVING early, that I should make new friends—that was the whole reason why we came to TAC camp. So, she signed me up for an art class with kids my age.

When I got to the room, there were four other girls there. They were all chattering like squirrels, so I went up to them.

"Hello!" I said.

One girl said something to me that I didn't understand. I shook my head.

"I can't speak Chinese," I said.

"I wasn't speaking Chinese," the girl said to me, her eyebrows flying to her forehead, "I was speaking Taiwanese."

"I can't speak Taiwanese either," I said.

"You can't speak Chinese OR Taiwanese?!?" the girl said. "Why not?"

I didn't know what to say. Mom and Dad spoke to each other in Taiwanese and Chinese at home, but they always spoke to us in English. Once when a girl in my school asked me the same question, my teacher had answered for me.

"Your parents are Italian, right?" Mrs. Whitton had said to her. "Do you speak Italian?"

She had shaken her head, no.

"Well, then," Mrs. Whitton said. "Why should Grace have to speak Chinese? It's the same thing. You're both Americans, and in America we speak English."

I had been happy with that answer then, but now, my tongue felt frozen to my mouth and I couldn't say anything. The Chinese girl looked at me as if I were a filthy cockroach crawling on her food, her fat face wrinkled in disgust.

"I don't know," I mumbled.

"I know why," one girl said, her nose arching toward the ceiling. "It's because you've been Americanized. My mother says she would never let me become Americanized. She said that when you're Americanized you don't have any culture."

the mean girl

100

"You're a Twinkie!" another girl said. "My brother said Chinese people who are Americanized are Twinkies. Yellow on the outside but white on the inside!"

The girls cackled and jabbered at each other in Chinese like mockingbirds. I felt like a helpless fish frying in oil, with a red-hot heat burning my face and stinging my eyes. I turned around so they wouldn't see me cry.

More kids and the teacher came in. I breathed in my tears and sat down. We sat at small tables and the teacher put paper and crayons in front of us. I sat as far away from those girls as possible.

The teacher taught us a little bit about colors. She asked us to draw something red, so I drew a piece of watermelon. Then we had to draw something blue, so I drew a blue bird. Then she had us draw something

my drawings

white, and I drew a unicorn. Then she asked us to draw something yellow. But I couldn't think of anything yellow that I wanted to draw.

The teacher walked around the room and looked at everyone's drawings.

She stopped and looked at my drawings. "This is lovely," she said, looking at my picture of a bluebird.

She showed the rest of the class, "Look at the beautiful drawing of a bluebird that Pacy did."

All of a sudden I felt better. I didn't have to speak Chinese to be a good artist. But my smile disappeared when I saw one of the girls at the other table scowling at me.

The teacher kept walking around the room and I heard her stop at the girls' table and say, "Now this is nice and yellow. Is it a banana?"

The girls laughed. "No," I heard them say, "it's a Twinkie!"

Twinkie

mean girl's drawing

I pressed down on my crayon so hard that it broke. The hot oil inside of me was blistering and bursting. In my head I wanted to shout, "I never want to speak Chinese ever if it makes me mean like YOU!" But I didn't say anything.

When the class was over, I went back to our room and I threw myself on the bed. And then I cried and cried. I HATED, HATED, HATED those girls. They were so horrible. Ki-Ki saw me crying and ran to get Mom.

"What's wrong?" Mom asked me. "Did something happen?"

I shook my head. I didn't want to tell anyone what those girls said. But I kept crying.

Dad went and asked the art teacher if anything happened at the class, but the teacher said I had been fine. She even said I did very good drawings. I stopped crying and started hiccuping.

"Did she really say that?" I asked. Maybe things weren't so bad. I probably would never have to see those girls ever again. I blew my nose and rubbed my eyes. Then I asked Mom, "Why did you want me to have more Chinese friends?"

"Was someone mean to you in your class?" Mom asked. "What did they say to you?"

"No." I shook my head. I still didn't want to tell anyone what had happened. "No one said anything."

Mom sighed and sat next to me. "I thought it would be good for you to have friends from your own culture," Mom told me, "so you could know people who are like you. Did I ever tell you about my first friend in America?"

MOM'S FIRST FRIEND

When Dad and I first came to the United States, I was very lonely. Dad was in medical school and I was going to college. But I had never lived away from my family before. I was used to having my four sisters and brother, my parents, my grandparents, uncles, and aunties around everywhere. In Taiwan, we used to all eat dinner together, laughing and talking—everyone bubbling over like simmering soup. When I came to the United States, everything seemed quiet and cold. Usually, I ate dinner all by myself, because Dad was too busy. I would shiver on my way to school, the wind biting me the whole way. People would talk and laugh and walk by me as if I were an invisible ghost. I was scared to talk to them because my English was so bad. I didn't understand the TV or my teachers or anyone.

They all spoke so fast, their words sounded like monkeys jabbering. I didn't know how to make friends with any of them. I was sad and lonely and homesick. I felt like a thistle in a rose garden.

Mom in America

Every day I would come home from class and cry and cry. One day, while I was crying, someone knocked on the door.

"Are you okay?" someone called out in Chinese.

I was so surprised that someone was talking in Chinese that I stopped crying and opened the door.

At the door was a Chinese girl, with a grin like a melon slice. Her name was Mei. She had been visiting a friend next door and had heard me crying. When she learned I was Chinese, she decided to come over.

What a difference it made knowing Mei! We became fast friends. I clung to her like a vine and she supported me like a tree. She told me how she had been homesick, too, when she first came, but now she never wanted to go back. She introduced me to her American friends, helped me with my English and my studies. She never was impatient with my bad English or my fear of American things, because she had had them, too.

Slowly, I started to feel like the United States wasn't so bad. I stopped thinking so much about all the things I missed and started thinking about all the things I could do. I made more friends. I ate pizza. I went to the movies. America began to feel like home. And now it is.

"But that is why I wanted you to have friends from our culture," Mom told me. "Because it's easier when you know people who understand."

"But just because they're Chinese doesn't mean they're the same as me," I said. "I don't think they understand at all."

"That's true," Mom said. "But because they are Chinese they are more likely to understand. Look at you and Melody. Don't you think she understands?"

I nodded, but I wasn't convinced. "It's not fair. To Americans, I'm too Chinese, and to Chinese people, I'm too American. So which one am I supposed to be?"

"Neither and both," Mom told me. "You don't have to be more one than the other, you're Chinese-American."

"Or Taiwanese-American," I complained. "It's so confusing."

"Good thing you're so smart," Mom said. "You can keep it from getting mixed up."

"Yeah," I said. "But everyone's not as smart as I am."

Chapter 24

New York City

basket of crabs

SINCE IT WAS SUMMER, MOM AND DAD PLANNED for a family vacation after the conference. This time we were going to go to New York City.

I was always confused about New York City. Was the city named after the state or was the state named after the city? Whenever we told people where we lived, we had to say upstate New York, not New York. If we only said New York, they thought we were from New York City. I didn't think that was fair. New York City was a lot smaller than the rest of the state.

New York City meant Chinatown and that meant we could buy all the things we couldn't get in New Hartford. So, Mom did all her grocery shopping. She took us to a Chinese grocery store and told us to pick whatever we wanted.

The Chinese grocery store was cramped and

crowded and had a strange smell, kind of like the way your feet smell after you've walked in the rain. Lissy said it was because of the dried mushrooms in the window. There were blue crabs in a basket by the stairs and boxes and boxes of sunshine yellow mangoes and sand-colored Chinese pears on the floor. We had to pick things that could keep for a long time, so Lissy pulled out some canned lychees while I picked up a bag of Chinese Popsicles and Ki-Ki grabbed some Chinese New Year candy. When we brought the items to the cart, Mom told us to get more.

"Get three or four packs," Mom urged us. "They will have to last you the whole year."

By the time we finished picking out everything we wanted, we had two whole carts full of groceries. It took us a long time to

two grocery carts

check out, and Dad went to go get the car while Mom paid. The owner of the grocery store came out and helped us put the groceries in the car. He bowed to Mom and thanked her for coming. He gave Ki-Ki, Lissy, and me each a box of chocolate caramels for free! Mom said it was because we gave him such good business. And we had. The whole car was full and I had to sit on six cans of baby corn for the rest of the trip.

After we went grocery shopping, Mom and Dad brought us to a Chinese bakery for a treat. Dad ordered five diamond-shaped pieces of thousand-layer cake—one piece for each of us. It didn't really have a thousand layers, but it was soft, sweet, and very yummy!

thousand-layer
cake

"Can someone get a job eating cake? Like a professional cake eater?" I asked. It was August already and I still hadn't "found myself."

"No!" Mom laughed at me. "Anyway, you would get tired of eating cake all the time."

"I wouldn't," Lissy said. "I can eat cake every day. Breakfast, lunch, and dinner. The whole thing! Chomp! Chomp! Chomp!"

"You sound just like your uncle," Mom said. "He loves cake. Did I ever tell you the story about your uncle and the cake?"

UNCLE SHIN AND THE SPECIAL CAKE

Well, when we were kids we weren't very rich, so we rarely got anything special. Sometimes Grandma gave us little candies or cookies, but never anything much better than that. However, one day, a rich auntie came to visit us. She brought us a big box wrapped with a silky bow.

Do you know what was in it? There was a cake inside. We had never been lucky enough to have a whole cake before. It was a frosted white rectangle with sugary pink flowers and pastel green leaves. Every inch of that cake held a promise of sweet delight. My sisters, my brother, and I stared at it with big eyes and licked our lips. We wanted to eat it so badly! The worst was my brother, Shin, you know—Uncle Shin. He loved to eat and he usually got the best of everything. He was the only boy in the family, so Grandma spoiled him. "That's mine," he growled, like a starving wolf, his eyes devouring the cake. He wanted that whole cake for himself.

While my auntie was talking to Grandpa, Grandma took the cake into the kitchen. She cut it into eight equal slices. One slice for each of us. I couldn't wait. We crowded around her and inspected each slice to make sure they were all the same size.

Around the cake

Uncle Shin kept circling us as if he was a hunting tiger. "I want all the cake," he kept hissing. "I want all the cake. Give me ALL of it."

But just as Grandma finished slicing the cake, Auntie called out to say she was leaving. We all

110

had to go and say good-bye. We left the cake on the table and bowed good-bye to Auntie in front of the house. All of us said good-bye and waved, except for Shin. He had disappeared.

When we went back to the kitchen, there was Shin. He was devouring the cake like a hungry pig, crumbs and frosting decorating his mouth and nose. He was such a greedy boy and he was determined to have the whole cake to himself. But we had only left him alone with the cake for a minute, so he wasn't able to eat the entire thing. Do you know what he did instead? He SPIT on all the other pieces!

It was so gross; he ruined everyone else's piece so he could have it all. And he did. We watched him eat every piece. What a spoiled boy he was! But that night he had a horrible stomachache and no one felt sorry for him.

"I would have just eaten around where he spit," Lissy said.

"Ew!" we all said together. "Yuck!"

Chapter 25

Halloween at School

jack-o'-lantern

I COULDN'T BELIEVE THE SUMMER WAS OVER, but it was. The leaves turned as yellow as a Chinese pear and the air felt like it came from an open refrigerator. Too soon, it was time to go back to school. Lissy took the big bus to junior high school and Ki-Ki went with me to the bus stop. Ki-Ki was in kindergarten now.

My new teacher was Mrs. Piterassi. She was tall and had curly, short hair the color of cinnamon. Melody was in my class, and so was Sam Mercer. That made us happy. But Becky was in Mrs. Wynne's class, across the hall.

Mrs. Piterassi had been Lissy's teacher, too; she remembered that. On my first day she said, "Oh, I taught your sister Beatrice." I hoped she didn't think I'd be good at math like Lissy was.

Mrs. Piterassi was a fun teacher. If your birthday was on a school day, Mrs. Piterassi gave you a big lollipop. I was sad because my birthday was on a Sunday this year, so I wouldn't get a lollipop. But for Halloween she let me draw a big picture of a laughing jack-o'-lantern and she taped it on the window.

Mrs. Piterassi also said that we could have a costume contest for Halloween. That was exciting. She said we should all wear our costumes and she would get some of the other teachers to judge who had the best costume.

"What should my costume be?" I asked everyone. I spent a lot of time drawing myself in different costumes. I drew myself as a silver fairy, a princess dressed in velvet, an amethyst butterfly, and a green-faced witch, but I wasn't sure if I wanted to be any of them.

No one helped me come up with more ideas. Lissy said I should go as a "Thing," like her. That meant painting your face pasty green, putting on a shower cap, and wearing Dad's doctor gown. She always went as a Thing.

"No one knows what you are when you go like that," I complained to her.

"That's why you should do it," Lissy said. "You'll be the only Thing in your class."

I wasn't convinced. Being a Thing was not my idea of a good costume.

Most people were buying their costumes from the store. We went, too, but I didn't see anything I liked. I didn't like the masks that came with the costumes; they were hard plastic with cheap colors and fake smiles. And you just tied the masks around your head with a rubber band. They didn't look *real*. I realized that if I wanted a good costume, I'd have to make it myself. But how? And what would it be? I could cut two eyeholes in a sheet and go as a ghost, but that seemed boring. Besides, not only would Mom not like it if I cut holes in a sheet, but we didn't have any plain white sheets. We had ivory ones with printed coral red flowers, and coffee-colored sheets with stripes, and canary yellow ones with floating balloons—but no plain white ones. What kind of ghost would have flowers printed on her? I kept walking around and around.

Finally, when Ki-Ki said she was going to be the Wicked Witch of the West, I got an idea. I'd be a black cat! I could wear Lissy's old black dance leotard and I could make cat ears and tape them onto a headband. I could even draw whiskers on my face with Mom's makeup pencil.

me as a black cat

When I got home, I told Mom my idea. She agreed that it was a good one. We opened up Lissy's old clothes drawer and found the black leotard. I tried it on and it fit! "But we have to buy you new stockings," Mom said, holding up Lissy's old ones. "These have holes and runs in them."

I couldn't wait for Halloween after that. I made Ki-Ki and Lissy promise not to tell anyone what my costume was. I didn't even tell Melody.

"What are you going to be?" I asked Melody.

"It's a surprise," she grinned and said. "What are YOU going to be?"

I shook my head, too, and kept my lips tightly closed. It was SO hard to keep it a secret! I could feel it wanting to burst out of me like a popping balloon.

On Halloween, Mrs. Piterassi let us change into our costumes. The girls went into the girls' bathroom and the boys went into the boys' room. I drew on my whiskers, colored my nose with the black makeup pencil, and wiggled into my new stockings and leotard. But when I looked down at my legs, they were the wrong color! Bad luck! Mom had bought me navy blue stockings instead of black ones by mistake!

I didn't know what to do. Should I take the stockings off? Then I'd be a black cat with pale legs. And I'd be cold. But now I was a black and blue cat. Whoever heard of a black and blue cat before?  But without the stockings, it probably wouldn't even look like a costume. I'd look like a ballet student with cat ears. I decided to leave the stockings on. If anyone asked, I'd just say I meant to be a black and blue cat.

Sam Mercer as Santa Claus

It was fun seeing everyone's costumes. There were lots of monsters and ghosts—I was glad I hadn't gone as a ghost. Sam Mercer was Santa Claus, and he had made his beard from notebook paper he cut into shreds. Another boy was a robot made from a box covered with tin foil. But the funniest one was Melody! She had cut a hole out of a laundry basket and put it around her waist. Then there were clothes filling the basket. "I'm a basket of laundry!" she told us.

Melody as laundry

Everyone's desks were laid out for a party. At each desk there was a cup of apple cider, an orange frosted cupcake with black and brown sprinkles on it, some candy corn, and an apple! Mrs. Piterassi was playing some creepy music. Some other teachers were sitting at the big table, ready to judge our costumes. We paraded around them before we sat down.

When they announced the winners, Melody won first prize! Mrs. Piterassi gave her a blue ribbon and a huge lollipop with rainbow colors twisted into it. Sam Mercer got honorable mention and a bar of chocolate with a yellow ribbon on it. I didn't win anything. The judges must have noticed my blue legs. Maybe if my legs had been black I might have won something.

On the bus ride home, Melody let me lick her lollipop.

"You're so lucky," I told her. "You won the blue ribbon, a lollipop, and you got to stand next to Sam Mercer."

"You're lucky, too," Melody said. "It's OUR lucky year, remember?"

"You're the only one who won the ribbon," I said, "so you're the only lucky one."

I looked out the window. I felt like one of the early falling leaves, brown and dried up and turning to dust in the blustering wind.

"I'm not lucky," I told Melody. "I'm not lucky at all."

Chapter 26

A Prize

turkey

AFTER HALLOWEEN, WE TOOK DOWN THE JACK-o'-lantern picture and hung up pictures of pilgrims and horns of plenty. I drew a big turkey with purple and red feathers and Mrs. Piterassi put it on the bulletin board next to the calendar.

"November, December . . ." Melody counted the months, "the year is almost over!"

"I know," I said sadly, "and I haven't found myself or my talent. I guess I'll have to wait until the next Year of the Dog."

But, the next morning, while we were all sitting in our seats, the loudspeaker crackled. It was a surprise announcement.

"I would like to congratulate one of our students—Grace Lin," Mr. Hargraves, the principal, announced through the loudspeaker.

Everyone turned around and looked at me. What had I done?

"Grace's book, *The Ugly Vegetables*, has won fourth place in the National Written and Illustrated Awards Contest for Students. This is a great

my book

honor, especially since she was chosen out of more than 20,000 entries. Grace will receive $400 and a certificate for winning fourth place."

I couldn't believe it! I felt like I had been tickled awake from a nap. Melody was bouncing up and down in her seat. The whole class was clapping. I had forgotten about the contest over the summer and now I had won fourth place!

"Congratulations, Grace!" Mrs. Piterassi said. All my friends gathered around me, congratulating me. I couldn't wait to go home to tell everyone.

At home, Mom and Dad were just as excited as everyone else.

"You said you'd cry if my book won a prize," I reminded Mom.

"Oh yes," she said, and she hid her face in her hands and pretended to cry.

Dad put his hands over his face and pretended too. Ki-Ki and I laughed. Lissy rolled her eyes. "Can we stop now?" she groaned. "It only won fourth place. It won't get published."

"But it won $400!" Ki-Ki said. "You're rich!"

Suddenly, like the last piece of a puzzle fitting into place, I realized something. I was rich. And not only was I rich, I had won a prize. I had talent as an author and illustrator. I finally knew what I could do when I grew up—I could make books. When I grew up, I could have a whole shelf of books all written by me. I *was* lucky. Like a creamy chocolate in my mouth, a warm feeling melted through me. I smiled my biggest smile.

"I found myself!" I told everyone. "I'm going to make books when I grow up."

"Yeah, right," Lissy said. "You'll change your mind."

"No, I won't!" I insisted. "You'll see."

"There's lots of time to find out," Dad said. "There's no rush."

"Yes, there was," I told him. "I had to figure it out before the Year of the Dog was over."

"Oh!" Dad said, laughing. "Well, I'm sure all the dogs in the world are now satisfied."

Chapter 27

American Holidays the Chinese Way

Mom's mashed
sweet potatoes

ON TV, AFTER SOMEONE GETS RICH, EVERYTHING changes. They get servants and fancy clothes and big houses. After I got rich, none of these things happened. Mom said I'd have to get even richer for those things.

But I didn't mind, because I had figured out what I wanted to do when I grew up. And just in time. Snow fell from the sky like clumps of white rice—the holiday season was here!

Thanksgiving and Christmas are two of the most important holidays in the United States. It took Lissy, Ki-Ki, and me a long time to show Mom and Dad how to celebrate them right.

Every year for Thanksgiving we had to talk Mom into buying a turkey.

"Why don't I get a chicken?" Mom would say. "A turkey is too big."

"No!" we would all say in unison. "You HAVE to eat turkey on Thanksgiving."

"Okay, okay," she said. "But you have to eat the leftovers. Dad and I don't like turkey."

Then Mom would rummage through the frozen food section, trying to find the smallest turkey possible.

Lissy tried to talk Mom into making mashed sweet potatoes, like they do on TV. Mom made them, but she didn't put them in a bowl like Americans did. She molded them into small cakes and then decorated them with herbs. They were like marigold-colored cupcakes with parsley sprinkles. We couldn't help but laugh when we saw them.

"What?" Mom said. "Aren't they prettier this way?"

Thanksgiving dinner at our house was always like that. We always had a lot of food covering the whole table. But it was full of glassy rice noodles, stir-fried shrimp, crispy fried fish, meaty dumplings, tangy sweet and sour pork, thick egg drop soup, white rice, and a very small turkey. The turkey was never in the middle of the table, but

turkey

Our Thanksgiving Dinner

always on the side, because Mom only made it because we said we had to have it.

"The pilgrims didn't eat like this at the first Thanksgiving," Lissy said.

"They probably never ate Chinese food ever!" I said.

"Ah, but if they did," Dad said, "I bet this is what they would've wanted for dinner."

Christmas was the same way. Everyone in our neighborhood hung up Christmas lights all over their houses and trees. We tried to get Dad to do the same. Dad hung the lights, but he didn't spend too much time doing it. Without putting on his coat or boots, he ran outside and threw them on a bush.

X-mas lights at our neighbor's house

"Brr," he said, stomping the snow from his bedroom slippers, "it's cold out there."

So, of course, while everyone else's lights were in nice arches and

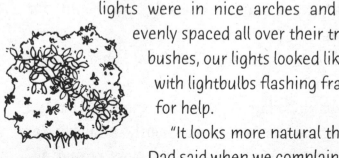

X-mas lights at our house

evenly spaced all over their trees and bushes, our lights looked like a blob with lightbulbs flashing frantically for help.

"It looks more natural this way," Dad said when we complained. "If a bush were ever to grow electric, rainbow-colored, blinking lights, I'm sure it would look more like our bush than anyone else's."

And Mom hated buying a Christmas tree.

"The poor tree," Mom would say. "Do you know how many years it took for that tree to grow that big? And you want to cut it down just to decorate it for a couple of weeks? How about we just decorate my rubber tree plant? It is almost as big as that tree."

They didn't understand at all!

But they did get us Christmas presents. Chinese people usually don't give gifts; they give lucky red envelopes of money. Mom said it was much more practical that way. But we told them that for Christmas we were supposed to get presents.

"But it's the same as if I give you money," Mom would argue. "What's the difference? I buy it for you or you buy it for yourself."

We just shook our heads.

"Okay," Mom said, "what do you want for Christmas?"

Now, this was more like Christmas! Hmm . . . what did we want?

Lissy wanted clothes. Now that she was almost a teenager, she wanted to be stylish—probably for boys. I thought clothes were the most boring gift

124

ever. Ki-Ki wanted more toy ponies. Her friend Sandy Pan had 100 ponies. Ki-Ki only had four. She wanted to catch up with Sandy. I didn't think Mom would buy her ninety-six ponies, though.

"What about you, Pacy?" Mom asked.

I thought hard. At first, I thought maybe I wanted some new paints and drawing paper. Ever since I decided I was going to write and draw books, I needed a lot of supplies. But, somehow, that didn't seem special enough to be a Christmas gift. In books, Christmas gifts were always fancy toys or games. So, I thought about what kind of toy I wanted. At school we were reading about a pioneer girl. She had a doll with a bonnet and a cornflower blue calico apron. It had a rag body and a shiny clay head with painted blue eyes and black hair. They had called it a china doll. I decided I wanted one of those, so I could pretend I was a pioneer girl.

pioneer china doll

"I want a china doll," I told Mom. "You know the kind of dolls with the head made out of clay? I want one of those."

Mom nodded her head.

On Christmas morning, we were all excited to get up. Even though we already knew what our presents were, it was fun running to go open them. Lissy got a new pair of jeans and the peacock green and blue striped sweater she had wanted. Ki-Ki got a lavender-colored toy pony with sparkling fake jewels on it. But I got a Chinese doll. It wasn't anything at all like what the pioneer girl had. It was a Chinese woman with long black hair wearing a pink silk dress and carrying flowers. I was so disappointed.

China doll
Mom gave me

Mom came down to see us open our gifts.

"What's wrong?" she asked. "Isn't that what you wanted?"

"But I asked for a china doll," I said. "You know, with the clay head."

"But it is a Chinese doll," Mom said, "and her head is made out of porcelain. I even ordered it from China."

It took a little while to explain. Finally Mom said, "I'm sorry it wasn't what you wanted, but do you like the doll anyway?"

I looked at the doll. She had a nice face. It wasn't her fault she wasn't the same as the pioneer girl's.

"Oh well," I said, "I guess I can pretend I'm a pioneer girl in China."

Chapter 28

Here Comes Chinese New Year!

upside-down luck
New Year decoration

THE ONE HOLIDAY MOM AND DAD DID KNOW how to celebrate was Chinese New Year. Sometimes we thought they celebrated it too well, especially when Mom made us clean.

"Pacy, clean the mirrors," Mom would say. "Lissy, vacuum the carpet. Ki-Ki, polish the furniture. Everything has to be clean for Chinese New Year!" And we would have to sweep and mop and brush and polish everything. We were glad when we were finished.

cleaning the mirror

After that, Mom and Dad took out their Chinese New Year decorations. Mom hung up a bright red sign with a black Chinese symbol on it upside down on our door.

"It says 'good luck,'" Mom told us. "Hanging it upside down means good luck has already come in."

Mom took us shopping for new clothes. "Everything has to be new for the New Year," she told us. "Oh, and I have to cut your hair, too!"

Mom always cut our hair as part of the New Year tradition. We had to cut it the day before New Year's because it was bad luck to cut your hair on New Year's Day. Mom had us sit on the high stool in the kitchen and put a big, white plastic cloth around our necks. Then she would wear her red and green plaid raincoat, take out her scissors, and cut our hair. Lissy wanted to get her hair cut at a fancy salon in the mall, but Mom said it was too expensive.

"But I want it to look good," Lissy pouted.

"They cut it just the same," Mom said.

"No," Lissy said. "A girl in my class says they cut her hair in layers."

"That's American hair," Mom said. "You can't cut our hair in that special way, it's too straight."

"But if you cut it," Lissy said, "it'll look just like Pacy's and Ki-Ki's hair. I'm older, mine should look different."

"Okay, I'll cut it differently," Mom said. "Did I ever tell you about the time they cut my hair in school?"

HAIRCUT AT SCHOOL

Do you remember how I told you that the schools in

Taiwan were different from here? Every day our uniforms had to be crisp and spotless, and our hair had to be straight and combed and NEVER longer than our ears. They were very strict about these rules. Every day when we entered the school building, a teacher waited at the door to inspect us. She was a horrible woman. She had a long, sharp nose like a knife and her hair was pulled back so tightly that it looked like it was painted onto her skull. She was always watching and waiting, her eyes scanning for any imperfections.

School inspector

My hair always grew so fast. Grandma had to cut it all the time, much more than she cut my sisters' hair. I hated getting my hair cut; I always felt like it was such a bother.

But one day, on my way to school, I touched my hair. It was just a little bit longer than my ears. But it was longer by such a small amount that I ignored it. I thought the teacher wouldn't notice.

But as I got closer to the school, I began to feel nervous. I could see her at the door, studying the line of students the same way a hungry cat would study a line of mice. I fluffed my hair up, hoping that would make it look shorter.

I saw a group of girls in front of me. I joined them, staying at the back. I hoped that they would hide me.

But they didn't. As I walked through the door, the

teacher pointed at me! She pointed at me with a stern face that seemed to be made of steel.

"No," she barked at me, like an army sergeant, "your hair is too long."

I felt like a fish trapped under frozen water as she reached into her pocket and took out a pair of scissors. She seized a handful of my hair and I felt the cold metal points on my neck ... Snip! Snip! I saw my hair flutter down to the ground like a dying moth. "Go," the teacher said.

Like a rabbit hearing a gun fired, I jumped away. While I hurried away from her, I touched my hair and I almost stopped still from shock. She had only cut one side! One side was cut very short, above my ear, while the other side was below my ear. It was lopsided! I looked so ridiculous. For the whole day, I had to have that bad hair cut.

Mom's haircut

Mom finished, "As soon as school was over, I ran all the way home so Grandma could cut it all one length."

"That's not the kind of different I mean," Lissy said.

"I know," Mom said.

When Lissy's hair was done, I thought it looked the same as always. But Mom got a curling iron and curled her bangs and brushed them out. Lissy's hair was all fluffy, like a poodle's. But when Lissy looked in the mirror she was happy.

Chapter 29

Good-bye, Year of the Dog

crate of
oranges

THAT YEAR, MELODY'S FAMILY WAS COMING OVER
to celebrate Chinese New Year with us. Since it was
on a Friday, we were all going to stay up late to welcome the New Year.

So Mom chopped and baked and steamed twice as
much as she did last year. We all had to help her in the
kitchen or she would never have gotten everything
done in time.

That year, I made dumplings. They weren't too hard
to make. Mom did all the hard parts. She rolled the
dumpling skins and made the filling. I cut the circles
out of the dough using a cookie cutter. Then I
spooned in the filling and folded the skin. My
dumplings looked like little half moons.

When we finished making the dumplings, Mom
boiled and fried them. Then, I peeled the shrimp

while Mom fried the fish and Lissy chopped some garlic. Dad added the extra part to the table to make it longer, and Ki-Ki filled the New Year tray all by herself. This time we had more things to fill it with. Ki-Ki put in Chinese New Year melon candy, honey noodle cakes, and red melon seeds, as well as M&M's.

I set the table, Ki-Ki took out the polished serving spoons, and Lissy scooped rice out into a big bowl like she was shoveling snow. Dad got out his special wine and the delicate wine glasses that were like soap bubbles with stems. All the while, with sizzling oil and vegetable slices popping in front of her like firecrackers, Mom kept frying and chopping.

Then it was Chinese New Year! The phone started ringing and then the doorbell rang. Melody's family came in. "Gong xi gong xi! Xin Nian hao!" they said. "Happy Chinese New Year!"

Melody's parents handed Dad a big plant. Melody and Felix handed me a big wooden crate overflowing with oranges. There were a lot of oranges. They kept jumping out of the crate, like rabbits trying to escape.

Melody's family at the door

"Why'd you get us so many oranges?" I asked. "We're never going to be able to eat them all."

"It's to bring you good luck, don't you know?" Melody told me.

"Not luck," Felix corrected her. "Money. The Chinese word for oranges sounds like the word for wealth."

"I'm glad I'm already rich, so I don't have to worry about it," I said.

"Then give the oranges back," Melody told me. "Then I'll get rich, too."

"Hey, me, too!" Felix said. Ki-Ki and Benji joined in as well.

We peeled the oranges and shared them. I guess it was a good thing they had brought so many. That way, everyone could get rich.

"Time to eat!" Mom called.

Everyone hustled into the dining room and then stared in awe. Mom had made so much food, even more than last year. This year we had clams that looked like ocean stones, a roasted duck with its head still on, fried rice with pink shrimp, steamed buns that looked like enormous marshmallows, pan-fried fish, jade green cabbage, golden brown dumplings, red marinated pork, and brownish black seaweed.

"Yum!" Felix said. "Let's eat!"

"The Year of the Dog is over," Dad said as he poured the drinks. All the adults got special Chinese wine while the kids got juice. When Mom wasn't looking, Lissy tasted the wine. She

wine

made a face when she drank it.

pig

"Now it's the Year of the Pig," Mom said.

"My year," Lissy added.

"You're a pig! You're a pig!" Melody and I laughed. "Oink! Oink!"

Lissy stuck her tongue out at us, but for once she couldn't think of anything to say back.

"The Year of the Dog was a good year," Dad continued, "don't you think?"

I thought about it. The Year of the Dog was the year that I met Melody and she became my best friend. It was the year I had won a prize, discovered my talent, and got rich. It was the year I had found myself and decided I was going to make books when I grew up. The Year of the Dog had been a great year.

"Let's give a toast to the Year of the Dog!" Dad said.

We all raised our glasses and clinked them together.

"Good-bye, Year of the Dog!" I said. "Good-bye!"

❀ A Note from the Author ❀

Dear Readers,

Twelve years! That is how much time has passed since this book, my very first novel, was published. So much has happened in the world and in my life—and probably in yours, too!

When this book was first published, I said that I wrote it because it was the book I wished I had owned growing up. As a child, some of my favorite books had been the "B" Is for Betsy series by Carolyn Haywood. In those books, Betsy goes to school and eats dinner with her family. She has fears, learns new things, and makes new friends. She's a regular girl, living an ordinary life, and I wanted to write something just like that—but this time, with someone that looked like me in it. As one of the few Asians in an almost all-white community, Betsy's world was sometimes too much like my own—a place that had everything I knew in it, except for myself. Writing *Year of the Dog* was, perhaps, a way to claim my own existence.

But, while all that was true, I also wrote *Year of the Dog* because I hoped people would like it.

I wasn't sure if anyone would. Maybe kids didn't want to read about the life of an Asian-American girl. Maybe readers would find it boring. Maybe they would be mad that the book wasn't about a dog.

Thankfully, my worries proved unnecessary. People read *Year of the Dog*, and most of them liked it (though some people did get a little upset that the book didn't have any dogs in it)—and some liked it a lot! So much so that the book is still being read, twelve years later.

And while I would love to take credit for the book's longevity, I don't think I can. I'm pretty sure the reason why the book has seen another Dog Year is because there are just some sentiments in life that are timeless. My favorite part of *Year of the Dog* is how it is peppered with stories about my parents and their lives in Taiwan. Even though those stories happened "a long time ago" and in an unfamiliar place, readers still connect. All kids know the feeling of being lonely, finding a friend, and being embarrassed by their parents. Friendship, family, and finding oneself are themes that everyone can understand.

Which is why, even though I wrote this book for myself, I am grateful that it is being read by so many. As I mentioned above, so many things in the world have changed in the last twelve years—some good and some bad. But whenever all the differences start to make me feel unhappy, I like to think about the readers of *Year of the Dog*. If so many of you can laugh, smile, and enjoy my little book—a book that I wrote because I felt like an outsider—then it must mean we have more things in common than not. A comforting thought I hope for all of us, and one that I truly thank you, my dear reader, for.

Happy Year of the Dog!

Best Wishes,
Grace Lin

Reader's Guide

blue ribbon

1. When does Chinese New Year (Lunar New Year) occur? Is it the same day every year? How is Chinese New Year different from New Year's Day (January 1)?

2. What are some of Grace's family traditions? Why are these traditions important to Grace and her parents? Does your family have any special traditions?

3. Grace and Melody quickly become best friends. Do you think this is because they are both Taiwanese-American? How do their similar backgrounds help them become such good friends?

4. Grace and Melody thought that their science fair project proved that plants prefer soda over water, milk, and orange juice, but Mr. McKnealy pointed out that their experiment was flawed because the plants were not kept in a controlled environment. Have you ever thought you made an important discovery, only to be proved wrong? Did Grace and Melody learn anything from their experiment, even though it was flawed?

5. Grace's mom tells her that the Year of the Dog is the year that people are supposed to find themselves. Grace spends the whole year trying to discover her talent. It is not until she wins a prize for her book that she realizes she wants to be an author/illustrator when she grows up. Do you think she would have still discovered that if she had not won a prize?

6. Grace is excited to try out for the part of Dorothy in the school play, until one of her classmates tells her that there can't be a Chinese Dorothy. Grace is very discouraged and doesn't try out at all. Do you agree that Grace shouldn't be Dorothy just because she is Asian? How would this make you feel if you were Grace?

7. Grace's mom tells her many stories from her childhood. How was her childhood different from Grace's? Ask your parents about their childhoods. How are they different from yours?

8. Grace is quite interested in the symbolism of the Year of the Dog. Because dogs are loyal, true, and friendly, the Year of the Dog is a good year for friends, family, and being "true to yourself." Find out what year you were born according to the lunar calendar. What are the characteristics of that year? Do these words describe you well?

9. Grace is made fun of because she can't speak Chinese or Taiwanese. Why do you think the girls made fun of her? Do you think this was right? How would you feel if you were Grace?

Here are some of the questions I used to interview my relatives. Maybe you can use them to interview your relatives, too. I hope they bring up some great stories!

1. Do you remember the most delicious thing you ate as a child? Tell me about it.
2. Who was your best friend as a child? How did you meet? Did you ever fight? What did you fight about?
3. Do you remember your first day of school? Were you happy or scared? Why?
4. Did you ever get in trouble in school? Did any of your siblings? What happened?
5. What did you eat for lunch at school? What was your favorite/least favorite lunch to get?
6. What was your favorite holiday as a child? What did you like best about it? Why?
7. How did you and your husband/wife meet? Can you describe the first time you saw each other?
8. Do you remember your wedding? What was the funniest thing that happened at your wedding? Or the most surprising?
9. Who was the first person in our family to come to the United States? Why did they come?

Extra Stories

To write my Pacy Lin books, I mined the memories of my parents, aunts, uncles, and grandmother for stories, interviewing them for hours. To add to the stories I already knew, I began asking them leading questions, like, "What was the most delicious thing you ever ate when you were a child?" and, "How did you make your best friend as a child?"

Many of the stories they shared were delightful, but not all of them fit into my books. Here are some that never made it into print—until now!

This is a story my mother told me about immigrating to the United States:

My mother's passport photo (when she came to the US)

Leaving Taiwan

When Dad and I left Taiwan, it was still under martial law (when the military controls almost everything) and the government was very careful about who they let in and out of the country. We prepared for two years before leaving. Test after test had to be passed, form after form had to be filled out, and paper after paper had to be approved and stamped before we would be allowed to leave. But finally everything was completed, and we were going to the United States of America.

How carefully we packed! My father bought me my own suitcase just for my things. It was dark blue leather, the color of ocean waves before a storm, with a buckle in addition to the zipper to keep it closed.

Aunts, uncles, relatives from all over came to wish me a good journey—each bringing me a good-bye gift that I promised to take with me.

"Americans won't have this," an uncle said as he gave me flat packages of dried seaweed.

"Will they have rice there?" an aunt asked, pressing a bag of it into my hands.

"I heard it's cold," my cousin said, giving me thick pairs of socks.

Soon the pile of things that I wanted to bring with me was even larger than my giant suitcase! All my sisters and brother crowded around as my mother, my grandmother, and I tried to fit everything in. Clothes were layered with books, bags of tea were stuffed in shoes, and preserved plums filled a carefully wrapped teapot. Every corner of that suitcase was stuffed and jammed with everything anyone thought I might need in the faraway place of the United States of America. My father had to go buy a luggage cart with wheels just so I could move the suitcase.

At last, the day for me to leave came. Dad and I had to go through customs. But the line was much longer, and we were much more nervous. What if there is a mistake on one of the papers? we thought. What if the official sees something he didn't like? But the worst thing was that the official was checking everyone's luggage, too. I didn't know that was going to happen! With the long line of people watching and waiting, the official opened each person's suitcase and inspected every item inside.

Finally it was our turn. I watched as the official carefully read our papers, rechecking all the signatures and stamps. Then he opened our suitcases. He took out all the clothing, turning my pants pockets inside out and squeezing the rolls of socks. He shook my books open to make sure nothing was hidden between the pages. He opened the bag of rice and stuck his hand deep into the bag, watching closely as the grains fell from his fingers.

It was only when he found a pile of toilet paper inside the

small rice cooker did he look at me—back then in Taiwan, toilet paper was not in rolls but in little stacks, like tissues. As he held the heap of paper up, I heard snickers and laughter from the line behind me. Dad looked at me in disbelief, and I felt my cheeks burn red with embarrassment. My grandmother had put that in. She had been afraid that there would be no toilet paper in that strange land of America. Even though I'd told her there would be, she wanted me to take some "just in case." I agreed, a little bit because, deep down, I wasn't really sure. But now the official was holding the toilet paper in his hands suspiciously. He squeezed and flipped through it, even unfolding a few of the sheets until he was finally satisfied that it was simply toilet paper.

He looked at me again, gave a little laugh, and shook his head. By this time, the crowd behind us was laughing loudly. Everyone thought I was a silly girl, bringing toilet paper halfway around the world! I felt very stupid, but as he waved us through, even I had to laugh a little. It was ridiculous. And for a while after that, I could never pass a bathroom without thinking about that stack of toilet paper from Taiwan.

This is another story from my mother, about her difficulties adjusting to life in the United States.

My mother when she first came to the United States

Milk in Tea

Getting used to life in the United States was not easy for me. Both your father and I were able to come to America because Dad was going to medical school and I was going to college and we had both learned English in school in Taiwan. However, in the beginning, I still had a hard time understanding all the words around me. I always felt as if I were in a fog, unable to see or talk. When I finally started to get accustomed to things in America, it was like finally being able to see through a frosted window in the spring.

At that time, I was going to college and living in an apartment building. One day, my landlady, Mrs. Reese, asked me over for tea. She had asked me a few times before, but I had always said no. I'd always been too scared to spend time with Americans, too scared to try to understand what they said in their fast English. But this time, I agreed.

I had never been in Mrs. Reese's apartment before. She lived on the first floor, and I always passed her door when I left for school or came back. She was always very nice to me. In fact, she let me rent the apartment the second year for the same price—she said she liked having me upstairs because I was so quiet.

Mrs. Reese's apartment was much nicer than the apartment I rented from her. Her hallway was a light, shiny wood, but the room where she had me sit for tea had a white carpet. I worried about walking on it with my shoes, but there was no place for me to take them off and no slippers waiting at the door, like we always had at home. As I walked carefully, I passed a glass cabinet full of things—pink faded paper roses that had been dipped in wax, a swan that looked like it was cut from a diamond, a glassy-eyed doll with bright pink jewels in her hair, and golden bottles of maple syrup shaped like leaves. I thought maybe she used to work at a gift store.

I sat down gently on a black couch as Mrs. Reese brought

out the tea. On the glass table, she had already placed a plate with all kinds of cookies on it—some golden brown, shaped like flowers, with bright red candied cherries in the center, and others as wide as my two fingers and half dipped in chocolate and covered with pink, orange, red, green sprinkles. They were too pretty to eat.

Mrs. Reese handed me a cup for tea. It was a white-handled cup with red and yellow roses and gold trim. I wasn't used to holding a teacup with a handle. The cups for tea we had at home were small and earth-colored, and you could roll them in your hands to keep them warm. But still, the tea smelled welcoming, and I held my cup eagerly as the amber liquid poured in.

But then Mrs. Reese took another gold-trimmed and rose-painted container and held it out to me. "Milk?" she asked me.

Milk! What for? I thought. I shook my head, and then I watched, horrified, as Mrs. Reese dumped the milk into her own cup of tea. As she stirred, the clear golden-brown color turned muddy, the color of soap scum after cleaning rust. Yuck! What had she done? Mrs. Reese had ruined her tea!

I tried not to show my disgust, but it was hard. I couldn't help wondering if the milk would curdle in her cup—maybe even turn into cheese! No one in Taiwan would ever put milk in tea.

But it was then that I realized I was not in Taiwan anymore. I was in America, and if this was the way people drank tea here, then I would have to get used to it. Maybe

I should try it, I thought. I opened my mouth to ask for the milk, but no words came out.

"Would you like some sugar?" Mrs. Reese asked me, handing me a spoon with a bowl full of sugar.

Sugar? That was strange, too, but not as strange as milk.

"Yes," I said, feeling relieved that I could at least do this correctly. I proudly put in a spoonful and stirred. I took a sip. Not bad. I liked it better plain, but I could drink tea with sugar. And as I drank from my white-handled teacup, I felt like I was slowly on my way to becoming an American.

This is a story from my father, about his childhood in Taiwan:

My father's passport photo

Dad Almost Misses the Train

I was a very good student in school. My father had a job as a clerk at the government office, and the pay was very, very low. But he kept that job for one reason: with it, he could send his children to school for free.

And this was very important. To get an education in Taiwan, you needed to be able to pass entrance exams and pay school fees. Most people could not afford to pay, even if they could pass the exams. But with my father's job, as long as I passed the exams, I could go to elementary, junior high, and high school—even beyond.

But passing the exams was not easy. I had to study all the time, starting in elementary school. My sisters and mother had to take care of most of the chores, cooking and cleaning, so all the brothers could study. When I turned twelve, I passed an entrance exam that allowed me to go on to junior high school in Taichung. Only nine other students from my elementary school of six hundred boys had passed, so this was a very big deal. My family was very proud. We lived outside the city, so I had to take the long train ride to Taichung every day. It left at five o'clock in the morning and returned at six o'clock at night, but it didn't matter. No trip was too long for me to go to school.

On my first day, I was so excited and nervous. I had never ridden the train alone before. I woke up before the sun rose.

But I didn't wake up before my mother. She was already packing my lunch box. Rice, slices of radish, and a brown egg the color of tea. The egg had been boiled with soy sauce and meat to give it a special savory flavor, and it was a treat for my first day of school. I grinned.

But there were many other things I had to do to get ready for my first day of school. I had to wear my school uniform, a stiff beige shirt and shorts—it looked a little bit like what Boy Scouts wear in the United States. I also had to make a new notebook, taking large sheets of paper, folding them, and then carefully cutting them to make pages. I also had to have new books, paintbrushes, ink, and pencils.

Before I knew it, my mother was calling me to eat breakfast, and as soon as I swallowed the last mouthful of rice porridge, it was time for me to go. I didn't want to miss the train on my first day of school, so I quickly left the house.

It was only when I reached the train station that I realized I'd forgotten my lunch! What to do? I looked at the big clock. There should be just enough time, I thought. So as fast as I could, I ran home. As I burst into the kitchen, my sister looked at me in shock and horror.

"What are you doing here?" she said. "You're going to miss the train!"

"My lunch!" I said breathlessly.

"Mom ran to the train station to give it to you!" she said. "You'd better go!"

I didn't even stop to groan. I turned right around and ran back to the station. As I ran, I heard the whistle of the train. Oh no! I couldn't miss the train on my very first day! I ran as fast as I could, my bag slapping my back like a spanking. The train screeched its warning whistle, and I threw myself through the closing doors, sweating and gasping. I grabbed my own knees for support as I panted, exhausted. I had made it. But as the train began to move, I raised my head and saw my mother on the other side of the train window, waving good-bye with one hand and holding my lunch box with her other.

I asked my great-uncle what the most delicious thing he had ever eaten was, and he told me this story:

A farmer's field in Taiwan

Great-Uncle's Favorite Sugarcane

When I was a young boy, younger than Ki-Ki, the farmers nearby grew sugarcane. When I walked to school, I would pass the fields of sugarcanes, their thin, long leaves spilling from the tops of the stalks like water from a flowing fountain. The stalks grew taller and taller every day until I couldn't see above them, and every day my mouth watered for a taste of them.

But that sugarcane was not meant for us. We would be strictly penalized if we were found eating it. Back then, Taiwan was ruled by Japan, and the best sugarcane and rice were sent there. This field, with its jade-green abundance, was already designated to produce the finest sugar for the Japanese.

So the morning the heavy, thick smell of burning sugarcane filled the air, I was filled with rueful jealousy. The burning of the fields meant that the cane, with its dead leaves and waxy outer layer of the stalks burned away, was ready to be cut and harvested. With their large, sharp, curved knives, the workers would soon be cutting the canes and carting stacks of them to their city—away from here, away from us, away from me and my stomach!

And that is what happened. Not long afterward, on my way home from school, I saw a farmer loading a mountain of sugarcanes onto a cart. The pile was so large that I wondered if the buffalo would be able to pull it. The farmer must have thought the same thing, because he went to the front of the cart and urged the buffalo forward.

Creak! The wheels moved. The sugarcanes jumped and jostled as the buffalo heaved forward and began to pull the cart down the road. The farmer walked next to it, pushing the buffalo on.

And I walked behind them, my eyes on the knocking sugarcanes in the cart. With every rock and hole the cart rode over, the sugarcanes shifted more—some moving closer and closer to the edge. One cane seemed to be very dangerously balanced. One more jolt and...Bump! Yes! The sugarcane fell to the ground!

I grabbed it quickly and stole a glance at the farmer's back. He didn't turn around. He hadn't noticed me at all! I ran away as fast as I could, clutching the sugarcane in my hands.

As soon as I was well hidden from view, I sat down and began to peel it. It was hard and tough without a knife, my fingernails hurt, but I kept at it. Finally, I was able to remove a section of the outer stalk, revealing the pale, juicy fibers of the sugarcane. Then, holding the cane as if it were a long corncob, I brought it up to my mouth and chewed. At last! The sweet, sweet flavor of the sugarcane! It was the best thing I had ever tasted.

And lastly, this is a story from my Grandmother, when I asked her about her childhood friends:

My grandmother's passport photo

Grandma and Goldfish

When I was young, my family lived in the city. We were twelve people—my parents, my grandparents, my four sisters, three brothers, and me—and we all lived together. It was very crowded. It was so crowded that my grandmother decided that two of the children should go and live with our aunt and uncle in the country. They had a big house out there with no children—plenty of room for one or two of us. I don't know why I was chosen over my sisters, but when I turned seven, one of my brothers and I were sent to live with them.

It was interesting living in the country. I helped my aunt and uncle feed the pigs with sweet potato leaves, hand-make tofu and potato flour, and watch the rice as it dried in the sun. Sometimes we collected snails from underneath the leaves in the rice fields or frogs from the creek, trying not to slip on the wet rocks and lose our gathered treasures. It was a busy but pleasant life.

But when I was old enough to go to junior high, my parents called me back to the city. To go to high school, any high school, one had to pass very difficult examinations. The junior high school by where my aunt and uncle lived was not very good—most students were more interested in farming than learning, and the teachers were very relaxed. But the city school was considered very good with stern teachers and serious students. My parents felt I would be more likely to pass the high school entrance exam if I came back and went to junior high school in the city.

So I returned home—though it didn't feel like home. After years in the countryside it was strange to be in the city, where the people and buildings felt so crowded. Most of the time, I felt as if I were a duck trying to fly with pheasants.

I especially felt that way in school, and my classmates felt the same about me. I wore my uniform exactly the same way as everyone else, with my hair in the identical style, but somehow they all knew I was different. "Country girl!" they whispered to each other and snickered.

The one who snickered the most and the loudest was a girl nicknamed Goldfish. She was called this because her eyes were so large and stuck out a little—just like a goldfish. But I thought she was also called Goldfish because everyone followed her like a school of fish. She was the most popular girl there, and everyone did as she said.

So when one day I opened my desk at school and saw it full of rocks, I knew she was responsible. In the glance that showed me that my paper and brushes had been replaced by gray, rough stones, I heard the waiting silence around me. Goldfish and everyone else was expecting me to get upset and cry or yell. Well, I wouldn't! I would ruin their fun. I quickly erased the shock and embarrassment from my face and quietly closed my desk. I could feel Goldfish's big eyes staring at me as I took out the books and paper that I had in my bag, prepared for class, and pretended that I hadn't noticed the rocks. I smiled grimly to myself when a disappointed sigh spread across the room. The next day, the paper and brushes were returned and the stones were gone. The days went on as if nothing happened.

However, I remembered. When the teacher praised my high math score and Goldfish struggled with her algebra, I felt sourly satisfied. I might have been a country girl, but I was a country girl who was good at math! In fact, I was the best in the school—something I knew proudly as I carried my report card home.

So I was surprised when Goldfish meekly approached me after school.

"Do you think..." she started, and then, after a

hesitation, said, "Do you think you could help me with my math homework?"

I looked at her with my mouth open, like a waiting frog. Goldfish, who scoffed, teased, and tormented me, was asking for my help? Forget it! I was about to turn away without a word, but she grabbed my arm.

"I know you have no reason to help me," she said. "I'm really sorry about before, even though I know it's too late. I wouldn't have asked you, but I had to. I'm doing so badly that I might fail!"

I looked at Goldfish; her big eyes were pleading and full of tears. They reminded me of a baby rabbit caught in a trap. "Okay," I said to her, reluctantly.

Goldfish's face transformed with happiness. "Really?" she said. "Thank you! Thank you!"

Then Goldfish suddenly stopped smiling. She looked at me seriously. "You're a nice person," she said to me. "Now I'm honestly sorry about before, not just because I want your help in math, but because you're really nice. I promise, we're friends now."

And we were. I couldn't help forgiving and liking Goldfish. She was so loyal and true. She never went anywhere unless I was invited, too. She made everyone include me right beside her and lashed out like lightning if anyone even whispered "country girl." For the rest of junior high, she was my best friend, the best friend anyone could ever have.

*The following editor letter appeared in the advance reading copies (ARCs) of **The Year of the Dog** prior to publication:*

Dear Reader:

It is with great pride that I celebrate the publication of *The Year of the Dog* by Grace Lin. This is a very special book about friendship, identity, and finding one's passion in life, and for many reasons is exactly the book I wished I had growing up, and exactly the book I hoped to publish when I became a children's book editor.

There's a behind-the-scenes story of *The Year of the Dog* that you may find interesting. As childhood friends, Grace and I were two of the few Asian children living in our small town. We bonded over our love of books, and devoured any book with Asian American characters (at that time, there weren't many!). Grace and I remained close even after I moved away, and twelve years later, we were roommates just as we were both starting out in the children's book industry: Grace as a children's picture book author and illustrator, and I as an editorial assistant at Little, Brown. As the years passed, we both progressed in our careers, and at the same time, Grace's picture book audience was growing older and asking for older books. One day she told me, "I wrote a novel."

I read it in one sitting, and imagine my surprise and delight to find that I was a character in the book (guess who)! Many of the stories in this novel are based on events that really happened to us as children: our struggles with our ethnic identity, as well as school issues, friendships, and crushes—it isn't too often that an editor gets to work on a book that tells her story, too!

Everyone here at Little, Brown has fallen in love with *The Year of the Dog*; our publisher, David Ford, named it a publisher's pick for this season. It's both hilarious and poignant, and very powerful in its own way. I am thrilled to have played a role in introducing it to the world. Enjoy!

Sincerely,

Alvina Y. Ling

Associate Editor

A conversation over instant messenger with Grace Lin and her editor and childhood friend, Alvina Ling

Alexandre Ferron

Alvina: Hi, everyone, I'm Alvina Ling, currently Editor-in-Chief at Little, Brown Books for Young Readers, also known as Grace Lin's editor. Hi, Grace!

Grace: Hello! I think you should also introduce yourself as Melody, from the book, though.

Alvina: Ha! Yes, I'm Alvina Ling, aka Melody Ling from *The Year of the Dog*. Let's start off by telling people how we met. What do you remember about meeting me for the first time? How old were we?

Grace: Honestly, I don't remember how old we were, but I do remember my mom driving me over to your house. She was very excited and said that there was another Taiwanese family in the area. I wasn't sure how I felt about that—part of me was like, "big deal" and the other part was nervous, because I wasn't used to seeing other Asian people.

Alvina: Interesting. I think you had just turned ten, and I was about to turn ten, because it was the summer before fifth grade. My family had just moved to New Hartford, New York, from Edison, New Jersey. Edison was very diverse, and I don't think I realized yet that New Hartford was not at all!

Grace: I was so used to people being white that seeing anyone of color was disconcerting to me; a reminder that I, myself, was not white.

Alvina: Whereas I had lived in some places that were predominately white, and others that were really diverse, so I was used to both experiences. I remember that we were the same grade, and our older siblings were in the same grade, and then our younger siblings were a year apart. I have an older brother and a younger brother and no sisters, and I think I was jealous that you had two sisters. I think I also assumed that you would be really into feminine things, having two sisters, whereas I was what people used to call a tomboy back then.

Grace: Were you a tomboy? I don't think that occurred to me. I think I would've liked to be girly and feminine, but that wasn't really a thing in our house—I think my parents always stressed practicality and frugality! Which might explain my shopping habits now as an adult....

Alvina: Ha! My family was frugal, too!

Grace: I remember thinking it was neat that our families almost matched up, even that our birthdays were almost the same day: yours on the sixteenth of July, mine on the seventeenth of May. Even though they are completely different months, for some reason it was still cool to me then. I don't really think it's all that amazing now, but it does make it easy to remember your birthday.

Alvina: I think in the book *The Year of the Dog*, you made it so we were both born on the seventeenth, right?

Grace: Yes!

Alvina: What was your most poignant memory of us as kids?

Grace: Definitely the time when we were in seventh grade. All three elementary schools funneled into the junior high, and it was a big step for me—I felt overwhelmed by all the new people. I remember seeing you in a school setting for the first time as you stood on the stairs, and you waved at me and said, "Hi, Pacy!" and I felt so relieved and happy to see you, someone I knew...a friend!

Alvina: That's such a sweet memory! We had gone to different elementary schools, so seventh grade was the first time we were in the same school, even though we saw each other all the time at each other's houses. I remember feeling so happy to be going to the same school.

Grace: It's the same feeling I tried to convey in *Year of the Rat*, when Melody saves Pacy a seat on the bus. But, honestly, the biggest thing that I remember when we first met was your bedroom. It had the huge mural of all those animals. I was in awe and very jealous—which is why I had to include it in the book!

Alvina: I loved that bedroom! It had red carpet, which was my favorite color at the time. So, let's talk about how *The Year of the Dog* came to be! My family ended up moving out to California the summer after seventh grade. So we only ended up going to school together for one year.

Grace: Which is why *Year of the Rat* has the storyline of Melody moving away!

Alvina: That was such a bummer. But we stayed in touch and wrote letters back and forth all the way up through college. We lost touch for about two years—when you went off to Rome to study art, and then after I graduated I went to Taiwan to study Mandarin Chinese. And then finally we got back in touch because I decided I needed to move to Boston to try to break into book publishing, and my mother, who was still in touch with your mother, told me that you were living in Boston. I emailed you right away!

Grace: In the meantime, I had graduated from the Rhode Island School of Design and had been trying to get a book published. When you contacted me, I had just signed the contract for my very first picture book, *The Ugly Vegetables*.

Alvina: You suggested that we become roommates, so we did! I interned at your publisher, Charlesbridge, and also at the *Horn Book*, while working at B&N as a bookseller. You were working at Curious George Goes to Wordsworth [an independent children's bookstore] then.

Grace: Yes, we were both working at bookstores at the same time, too!

Alvina: And then I finally got a job at Little, Brown Books for Young Readers as an editorial assistant. I loved that we were both starting our publishing careers at the same time.

Grace: Yes, sometimes people—especially aspiring authors—think it's because I had you as a connection that my books got published. But, in reality, we both built our careers separately—though at the same time. It was only after we had both reached a certain level that we were able to collaborate.

Alvina: Right. And I think we tried to work together for years before it finally happened!

Grace: I even remember helping you choose your outfit for your interview at Little, Brown!

Alvina: I totally remember that! I borrowed a blazer from you. Of course, I interviewed in July and it was hot, so I never actually wore it, just carried it on my arm. Ha!

Grace: Did you? Now, why did I own a blazer? I don't think I ever went out of the house....

Alvina: It was probably a hand-me-down from your mom!

Grace: Yes! She probably thought I might need a power suit for something!

Alvina: Haha! Well, I was working at LBYR as an editorial assistant, and every time my manager, Megan Tingley, had a picture book text that needed an artist, I suggested you. She liked your art, but it never ended up working out. And then my division was being transferred to New York City, and right around then we were also starting to publish more middle grade and young adult, and I asked you if you had ever considered writing for older children. And you said, "Yes, actually! I have an idea."

Grace: I'd been trying to write a sequel for *The Ugly Vegetables*, but the picture book manuscript had ballooned to fifty pages. When you asked if I'd considered writing for older children, a bell begin to ring. Instead of cutting this fifty-page story into something to fit a picture book, why not let it grow as big as it wanted to and write it for older kids?

Alvina: I remember you wouldn't tell me what your idea was right away—but when you gave me a draft to read, it turned out to be all about our childhood friendship! So of course I loved it!

Grace: Well, it's funny to tell someone they are going

to be a character in your story. I thought it would be better to surprise you.

Alvina: I remember telling you it was too short, but that it was a good start!

Grace: Yes, you said it was too short and had no descriptions! I thought, "Oh, yeah, I have to write those, don't I?" Because as a picture book story it didn't need any—the pictures would be the description. I had to wrap my mind around the differences between middle grade and picture book stories.

Alvina: Did I say something like, "Add three descriptions to every page"?

Grace: I remember you said four descriptions to every page!

Alvina: Ha! Right before the interview, I actually tried to go back and find your first draft, but instead I found an email that said you mailed me the revision. Twelve years ago we worked on paper!

Grace: I know! I tried to find an old version, too, but it was recycled years ago!

Alvina: But I did find the memo I wrote to Megan asking if I could bring the novel to our acquisitions meeting!

Grace: Wow! I remember being so nervous about that— if Little, Brown would take it. I was living in Somerville, and our windows weren't insulated, and I remember shivering in the living room, checking my email just in case you had some news....

Alvina: I remember everyone loved it, especially our publisher at the time, David Ford. It was such a happy meeting! While we were working on it, I felt so lucky—because who else gets to edit a book where you're a character in the book?

Grace: I guess that could be a nightmare for some people!

Alvina: Haha! In the end, though, I knew I was really the only editor who could work on it. I remember one comment Megan had at the meeting was to add more conflict in the story, and I could suggest to you stories to add tension and beef up the book. For example, I knew your real-life story about not auditioning for Dorothy in *The Wizard of Oz*. You also added some tension by making changes to what really happened. So, for example, we had actually won the science fair in real life, but you changed it to have us lose, to add more tension! What were some of the other differences in the book compared to real life?

Grace: Well, one change is that I made us younger in the book, even though our ages/grades aren't necessarily specified. I did that because I kind of think we were really immature for seventh graders! Maybe everyone was a bit more immature back then (the clichéd "simpler times") but all the memories seemed more relatable to a younger audience. If I put us in junior high, I don't think people would have found us very believable!

Alvina: True!

Grace: Another change is our first day of meeting in the book, when the lunch lady accused you of stealing an extra lunch. That was not how we first met, of course, but the lunch lady did accuse you—do you remember that? That part was true!

Alvina: Yes, I remember that she confused me for you (or vice versa). You also had Melody dress up as a basket of laundry for Halloween. In reality, I dressed up as a pillow! It was the most comfy costume ever. I just pinned two pillows together and wore them like a sandwich board.

Grace: I was a black-and-blue cat, though, I know that!

Alvina: I remember that! I think it's fair to say that *most* of the events of the book are *mostly* true. And the spirit of the book is true to life.

Grace: Yes, just maybe a little out of order with some details tweaked.

Alvina: *The Year of the Dog* was your first novel, and your readers have come to be familiar with your inclusion of stories within the stories, both with these Pacy Lin books, as well as your fantasies, including *Where the Mountain Meets the Moon*. What inspired you to use this technique initially?

Grace: It wasn't really anything too thought out. Initially, I did it that way because it is easier for me to think and write in little stories—probably because I started as a picture book author/illustrator. But as time went on, I really enjoyed it. One of the things I like to do in my art a lot is put patterns on top of patterns—kind of an homage to Chinese folk art. Writing these little stories inside of the bigger story started to feel like an extension of that—patterns on top of patterns but using words instead of paint.

Alvina: That's a really cool way to describe it! Also, it must have been nice getting those stories from your family, too.

Grace: Yes, it was fun, but sometimes overwhelming. My parents, trying to be helpful, once went on a family reunion and decided to interview everyone to get "material" for me. After getting hours and hours of taped conversations, I realized there was an art to interviewing!

Alvina: Did you get any material in all those taped conversations?

Grace: Not really. I realized that to get stories you had to ask questions that would evoke a memory. The best stories came when I asked, "Do you remember the most delicious thing you ate as a child?"

Alvina: I love that question!

Grace: My parents' interviews were more factual—where were you born, what school did you go to? All interesting to a family historian but not useful to me, as I would probably just change all the names and dates anyway. Ah, fiction!

Alvina: I know my parents were a little jealous—they asked me when I was going to write a book about them!

Grace: We can write about your family next! The Melody Ling books!

Alvina: They would *love* that. Ha! Maybe in twelve more years. Do you remember anything about how you felt about the reception to the book's publication?

Grace: Well, I had published picture books before this—and all of them were mostly found in libraries or schools—rarely in stores, as being "Asian," they were kind of considered niche. So, I wasn't expecting too much from the novel either. But I remember one day going down an escalator in Barnes & Noble and I saw my book on display. I remember feeling so surprised and so...pleased! Like, wow, maybe I am an author now! I am really grateful that B&N got behind the book!

Alvina: I later discovered that the children's buyer at the time, Joe Monti, was a *huge* fan of the book, and put it on every promotion he could.

Grace: It made a world of difference! Honestly, it was the first book of mine that really made even a small splash.

Alvina: I remember when my sales director for B&N told me that it was being modeled in the stores! I was so excited. Since I used to work at B&N, I knew what a big deal that was. That they decided that every store should carry the book.

Grace: Which was a first for me!

Alvina: I was such a junior editor, though—looking back now, I realize how lucky we both were that it was so successful. Do you remember that there was a little Newbery buzz for the book? We were actually in Beijing together on vacation when the ALA announcements happened, so it was definitely not on our radar. But when I got back to the office, I remember Megan saying, "I'm sorry it didn't win!" and I was surprised that she thought it actually had a chance.

Grace: Yeah, definitely not on my radar then!

Alvina: So, looking back now on the publication of *The Year of the Dog*, do you have any wise observations to make?

Grace: It's funny, because having written other novels now, *Year of the Dog* is pretty different from other successful middle grade books. But I think it still works, because it has a lot of heart. And that just kind of happened by magic.

Alvina: It does still feel like magic now!

Grace: It does, doesn't it? All the way up to us still being friends!

If you love **The Year of the Dog**, *don't miss the sequel*
The Year of the Rat, *available now.*

Also check out Grace Lin's conclusion to The Year of the
Dog series,
Dumpling Days.

Keep reading for a sneak peek!

map of Taiwan
(not to scale)

"PINK, PINK, PINK," I SAID OVER KI-KI TO MOM. LISSY, Ki-Ki, and I were sitting next to each other on an airplane, and we were wearing the same hot-pink overall dresses, the color of the neon donut sign in the food court back in the airport. "Why did it have to be pink?"

neon donut sign

"That was the only color they had that was in all three of your sizes," Mom told me. "And I wanted to make sure you matched so it would be easy to keep an eye on you."

"I can keep an eye on myself," I said as I pulled at the brilliant-colored denim. The matching jumpers made it easy for everyone on the airplane to keep an eye on us, and it was embarrassing. Lissy thought so, too.

"I hope no one I know sees me," Lissy had said, horrified.

"I can't believe you're making me wear the same dress as a six-year-old."

"Seven!" Ki-Ki had said. "I'm seven!"

But Mom hadn't listened to even our loudest protests, and now we were on the plane in matching dresses. Whenever people passed us, they smiled and I didn't blame them. We looked ridiculous, like plastic birds in a flock of flying ducks.

"This is an important trip," Dad said. "Traveling is always important—it opens your mind. You take something with you, you leave something behind, 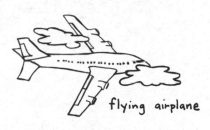 flying airplane

and you are forever changed. That is a good trip."

"Yeah, but why does it have to be a trip to Taiwan?" I asked. Dad always spouted in dramatic ways about things, sometimes to be funny but other times because he really meant it. When he meant it, we usually ignored him. "Why couldn't it be a trip to Hawaii? Or California? At least then we could've seen Melody!"

Melody was my best friend, and last year she had moved to California. I wished so much we were going to visit her. But, instead, we were going to Taiwan. Taiwan was far away. It was so far that I wasn't even sure where it was. Mom and Dad called it their homeland. But to me and my sisters, our small town of New Hartford, New York—with its big trees and sprawling lawns, the one shopping mall, and the red brick school with the tall, waving American flag — was our homeland.

our house in New Hartford

I was also grumpy because I had to sit in the exact middle of the row. Mom and Dad sat on either end, Lissy sat next to Dad, and Ki-Ki next to Mom. I was stuck between Lissy and Ki-Ki, and I didn't get to see anything that was going on. "What do you want to see?" Dad said when I complained. "There's nothing to see. You would be just as bored sitting on the end as you would be sitting in the middle."

"And I can't believe we're going to be gone for the whole summer," I said. It seemed so unfair. All my friends at school got to go to fun places for the summer, like the beach or amusement parks. Melody lived near the Universal Studios theme park. *They have a ride there*, she had written me. *It's even better than 3-D. They call it 4-D!*

"It's not the whole summer," Mom said. "It's just one month. Twenty-eight days."

"It's not like you have anything better to do," Lissy said.

"You don't, either!" I said. But she was kind of right. Even though I had other friends, ever since Melody had moved away, my school vacations seemed to drag on like waiting in line at the supermarket. But I still knew I'd rather be at home than go to Taiwan.

"I have lots of things to do," Lissy said with a superior look. "Why can't we leave earlier, like when Dad leaves?"

"I have to leave earlier because I have to work," Dad said before I could say anything to Lissy. "You are the lucky ones! I wish I could stay the whole time."

"Besides, we aren't staying that much longer," Mom said. "Just twelve days more. We want to be there for Grandma's birthday. She's going to be sixty, so it's important."

"Why?" Ki-Ki asked. Ki-Ki was always asking why. Ever since her teacher had told her that there was no such thing as a stupid question, Ki-Ki never stopped asking any. She used to even ask things like "Why is why, why?" Her questions weren't as silly anymore, but she still asked a lot of them.

"Well, remember how there is a Chinese twelve-year cycle—every year is named after a different animal, and it repeats every twelve years?" Mom said. "Grandma is going to be sixty, and that means she has lived through all twelve Chinese animal years five times. That is very lucky."

"Pacy and Ki-Ki, you've never been to Taiwan before. And

Lissy, you were probably too young to remember," Dad said. "We need to go to Taiwan so you will get to know your roots."

"Roots?" Ki-Ki said, swinging her legs to show Dad the bottoms of her feet. "I don't have roots!"

Lissy and I rolled our eyes. Ki-Ki still liked acting like a baby sometimes. Mom said it was because she was the youngest.

"Silly," Mom said. "You know what he means. We want you to see the place where we came from, before we came to the United States."

"You should know Taiwan. It's…" Dad said, his face dimming as he tried to think of the right word in English. His face fell, and he said it in Chinese instead. "It's…Taiwan is…bao dao."

Bao dao? I didn't know a lot of Chinese, but that word seemed familiar. It sounded like the Chinese word for …

jiaozi
(dumplings)

"Pork buns!" I said. "Fried dumplings? Taiwan is wrapped meat?"

"No," Mom said, and laughed. "You are thinking of baozi and jiaozi! I guess bao dao does sound a little like the words for pork buns and dumplings. But bao dao is completely different. It means 'treasure island.' People call Taiwan an island of treasure."

"Treasure?" Ki-Ki asked. "Is there buried gold there?"

"Well, no, not gold," Dad said. "Treasure like forests and water and rich earth to grow food."

Taiwan suddenly sounded like the woods in our backyard at home. Ki-Ki thought so, too.

"Taiwan sounds like camping!" she said. "Is that the treasure?"

I looked at Dad eagerly. Camping was interesting. We
had never gone camping. Dad didn't like it. He always said,
"What's so good about camping? Who wants to sleep on
the ground?" Maybe he would like it if we were camping in
Taiwan?

"No! Taiwan is not camping!" Dad said, and we could all
tell he was having a hard time thinking of how to explain it.
I was disappointed about the camping. "Taiwan is cities and
cars and culture and restaurants. In Taiwan, there are beds
and good food. A lot of good food!"

"So, food is the treasure of Taiwan?" I asked. I was still
thinking about the dumplings.

"Yes!" Dad said, and he and Mom laughed as if I had said
something very funny. "Yes, it is! Food probably is one of the
treasures of Taiwan. We will definitely eat a lot when we are
there."

I heard Lissy give a little sigh. I felt like sighing, too. I'd
have to last twenty-eight days in Taiwan until I could come
back home. That was so long. Already, it felt like forever.

"Don't worry," Mom said, watching us with a grin. "It will
be fun."

"Are you sure?" It wasn't that I thought Mom was lying; it was
just that sometimes her kind of fun wasn't the same as mine.

"Yes." Mom smiled. "You'll see."

Chapter 2

On the airplane

airplane window

BEING ON THE AIRPLANE MADE ME FEEL AS IF I WERE stuck in a plastic bottle. It was hard to tell if we had been flying for one hour or ten. At first, we played with the TVs. We all had our own — each was in the back of the seat in front of us, and we could watch any movie we wanted. At home, Mom let us watch only three TV shows a week. We'd each pick one and watch it together, which wasn't always fun. Lissy had just started choosing some silly hospital show with lots of kissing, and Ki-Ki liked a baby cartoon that we (even Ki-Ki herself) were all too old for. So I was excited to be able to watch whatever I wanted.

TV on the back of the airplane seat

But after a while, even that

became dull. I tried to read my books, but my head felt all stuffed up and I couldn't concentrate. Dad was right when he said there was nothing to see. The airplane ride was so long and so boring. It seemed as if the only thing I could do was sleep. Which I did, until Lissy elbowed me awake.

"They're bringing the dinner!" she said. A flight attendant was wheeling a cart and handing out prepacked meals to everyone. I turned the knob that held up my tray table on the seat in front of me. *Clack!* It fell open with a clatter, but no one paid any attention. Everyone was too busy getting the food.

Lissy passed down to me a tray full of covered containers all shiny and smooth. The largest container was wrapped with foil, which I carefully began to peel off. Getting airplane food was fun; it was like opening presents! Though not the most delicious-looking presents. Pale, flattened noodles and unknown meat chunks were drowning in the orange-brown overflow of curry sauce. A mix of sliced cucumbers, corn, and dark purple beans filled one of the small containers. The other container had faded melon cubes, the same color as unripe grapefruit. The dessert was in a wrapper with big white, fancy letters that said CHOCOLATE-CHIP SHORTBREAD, even though it was really just a chocolate-chip cookie.

airplane food

On the side were a napkin; a fork, a knife, and a spoon (all plastic); and a pair of chopsticks. Lissy pushed the chopsticks toward me.

"Since we're going to Taiwan," she said to me, "you'd better learn how to use chopsticks."

"I've eaten with chopsticks lots of times!" I told her. "I know how to use them!"

"No, you don't," Lissy said. "You hold them all wrong."

Did I? No one had ever taught me how to use chopsticks. I had just taken them and eaten with them the best I could. It had worked fine — I had always been able to get food to my mouth.

"Look," Lissy said. "You're supposed to hold them like this. Hold the top one like a pencil. They aren't supposed to cross over like that."

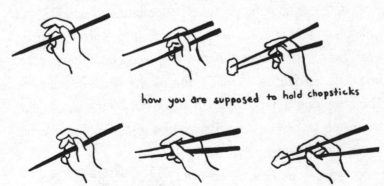

how you are supposed to hold chopsticks

how I hold chopsticks

I tried holding the chopsticks the way Lissy showed me. They felt awkward between my fingers, but I aimed them toward the container of cucumbers and corn and grabbed.

Plop! The slices fell from my chopsticks back into the tray like raindrops. I tried again. *Plop! Plop!* The cucumbers slipped off the chopsticks again.

"See!" Lissy said triumphantly. "You can't use chopsticks! I told you you're going to have to learn!"

"Speaking of learning," Mom said, leaning over, "I found out about a special cultural program they have in Taiwan. It's made just for kids like you — kids from America. We've signed you up for classes."

I stopped trying to pick up cucumbers. Classes sounded like school. Lissy thought so, too, because she made a noise that sounded like she was gargling mouthwash.

"Classes!" Lissy said. "But it's summer. It's vacation!"

"We want to make sure you don't get bored," Dad said.

Lissy, Ki-Ki, and I looked at one another. We all knew never to say we were bored when Dad was around. If we ever complained about having nothing to do, he always said something like "Let me give you some math problems."

"In Taiwan," Mom said, "a lot of kids study in the summer, too. But, anyway, don't worry. We just signed you up for fun classes."

This was another time that I didn't trust Mom's idea of fun.

"What kind of classes?" I asked.

"All different," Mom said. "Lissy has calligraphy, Pacy has painting birds and flowers, and Ki-Ki has paper cutting."

"I can cut paper!" Ki-Ki said. "I don't need a class for that."

"This is special paper cutting," Mom said. "You'll learn how to cut pictures out of paper."

"Isn't calligraphy Chinese words?" Lissy interrupted. "How can I paint Chinese words when I don't even know Chinese?"

"Yeah!" I said. "None of us speak Chinese! How can we take a class in Taiwan?"

"Remember, it's a special program. The teachers will be able to speak English," Mom said. "We were very lucky to find this. Remember that Taiwanese-American convention we went to with Melody's family a couple of years ago? It's run by a group like that. They want to make sure Taiwanese-American kids know about their culture. There is even a special boat tour, but that is for teenagers."

"I'm a teenager! Fourteen is a teenager!" Lissy said. "Why don't I go on that instead?"

"It's for older teenagers," Mom said. "High school."

"I'm almost in high school!" she said. "I could go!"

Lissy was still talking, but I had stopped listening. Lissy was always being boring about how old she was, like we would forget that she was the eldest. But besides that, hearing about the painting class had me worried.

I wasn't worried about actually painting. I was good at art. I wrote and illustrated a book that won four hundred dollars before, and I was going to write and illustrate books when I grew up. I had decided that a couple of years ago. I knew I would be able to paint fine.

But I remembered that Taiwanese-American convention Mom mentioned. Even though I had gone with Melody, I hadn't liked it. It had been horrible. The kids there were Taiwanese-American, and so was I, but they weren't like me at all. In New Hartford, now that Melody had moved, I was the only Asian girl in my class. I tried to be just like everyone else, and I always spoke English, even at home. But at that Taiwanese-American convention, all the girls there could speak Chinese and Taiwanese, and they called me a Twinkie. They said I had lost my culture. "You're yellow on the outside, but white on the inside!" one girl had said to me. "You're a Chinese person who's been Americanized."

And it was true. I was Americanized. In New Hartford, *Americanized* meant being like everyone else and having friends. But at that convention, it meant being humiliated and disliked. Was it going to be like that in Taiwan, too? Would everyone there make fun of me and call me a Twinkie? *Plop!* Another cucumber slipped from my chopsticks onto the tray, and I felt as if it were just like my heart falling.

Alexandre Ferron

Grace Lin

is the award-winning and bestselling author and illustrator of *The Year of the Dog*, *The Year of the Rat*, and *Dumpling Days*, as well as the Newbery Honor *Where the Mountain Meets the Moon*, *Starry River of the Sky*, and the National Book Award Finalist *When the Sea Turned to Silver*. Grace lives in Massachusetts, and invites you to visit her website at gracelin.com.